MW01174241

Jennifer Duncan

Sanctuary & Other Stories

Montreal, Quebec, Canada

DC New Writers Series edited by Robert Allen
(rena@netrover.com)
Book design and all photographs by Andy Brown
(conpress@ican.net)
Typeset in Gill Sans Condensed and Bembo

Canadian Cataloguing in Publication Data

Duncan, Jennifer, 1967–
        Sanctuary, and other stories

ISBN 0-919688-56-X (bound)
ISBN 0-919688-54-3 (pbk.)

        I. Title.

PS8557.U53824S35 1999   C813'.54   C99-901564-8
PR9199.3.D862S35 1999

The stories "Slice of Life" and "Camellia and Jane" have been
revised since their original appearance in *Blood & Aphorisms*.
"Slice of Life" was included in *The Stories of Blood & Aphorisms*.
The story "Confounding the Hounds" was first published
in *Matrix*.

DC Books
950 rue Decarie
Box 662
Montreal, Quebec
H4L 4V9

ACKNOWLEDGEMENTS

Thanks to my family, those here and those gone, for raising me to go my own way. Especially thanks to Kate Duncan, Rod Duncan and Sue Patterson for much-needed writing time at Last Straw Farm and Waupoos. Thanks to my teachers Barbara Walthers, Libby Scheier, Richard Teleky and Mary di Michele (who supervised this collection in its incarnation as a thesis). Thanks to the Ontario Arts Council. Thanks to the Banff Centre for the Arts and to Peter Oliva and Edna Alford. Thanks to my editor Rob Allen for choosing *Sanctuary & Other Stories* and helping me make it better. Thanks to all those who made me take deep breaths during the writing of this book — Anna Roosen-Runge, Elizabeth Gold, Jessica Argyle, Kent Wakely, Danielle Bobker, Sina Queyras, Steve Hall and Trish Salah and especially Rick Wahl, who brought me tea and tenderness. Thanks to my bro, Yukon Jake, for being my confrere. And thanks to all the old tribe, those who survived and those who didn't. Sorry, Davin.

DC Books acknowledges the support of the Canada Council for the Arts and SODEC for our publishing program.

THE CANADA COUNCIL | LE CONSEIL DES ARTS
FOR THE ARTS | DU CANADA
SINCE 1957 | DEPUIS 1957

for Davin
who died

TABLE OF CONTENTS

SLICE OF LIFE

With white hard joy I felt bones jutting at odd angles all around and inside me. Sharp, that's what I wanted to be, sharp like a sword dancer. I would stick a stiletto finger down my sickeningly slick throat and spasm up the acidic poison. Clean and sharp. Ninety-eight pounds strong. Addicted to coffee, my heart tapped staccato beats and I shook, quivered and raced my way around myself.

I looked dead. White bones caught in black fishnet. He was afraid to touch me, afraid the dry cold of my skin would burn, afraid his hand would be enmeshed in a web of bone, afraid I would crumble into dust. I stared at the pale, raised anarchy symbol he'd carved into his arm and I said, "You can't hurt me — stomp on my feet as hard as you can — harder." And looking deep into his eyes, I laughed as the combat boot stomped. The next day he was at the café with half a face. His left eye full of blood and his left cheek all scab, he sang, "Since my baby left me, I found a new place to dwell — Sunnybrook Hospital." and threw the table across the room as I ran out. He had taken four hits of acid and driven his motorcycle into a wall.

I breathed in short gasps but they filled my hollow form, rattling the bones with whirlwinds promising destruction. I stared at the freezing blue veins wriggling in my wrist. With a shudder, I turned the arm over and took off my watch. I held a razor blade delicately between my right thumb and index finger. The blade made my skin look very soft and young. I cut fifteen parallel lines in the tough side of my forearm, one for every year. I did not cut deep. The straightness of the red lines and the little, sharp, stinging pains were satisfying enough. But the blood would not flow. It only settled like carefully arranged pick-up sticks. Simone de Beauvoir said that women cut themselves to own the first carnal stab of the future lover, to prove they can hurt themselves better than he will. Too late for me. I just wanted to feel something, anything. Just wanted some proof that I was still alive — red wet blood, warm and flowing. Just wanted to open the scars that hid deep deep inside.

I cut strips of black cotton from the bottom of my t-shirt and twined them around my wrist. I vowed I would love and love would save me. PASSION or DEATH! My next lover had HATE with the E backwards carved into his inner thigh. The one after him stuck a needle in his arm every day. And the next one lost his job as a busboy because the customers complained about the blistery hive of cigarette burns on his arm.

Day after day I sat in the café as we all sat, moaning and cursing. Somebody killed herself and someone else got arrested and so-and-so died of a drug overdose. But this is not what concerned us. This is not what we bewailed in jaded conversation. No, it was nuclear arms and men in suits and poverty that quaked the ground under our feet and made us raise our voices and fists. It was concrete and tall buildings and telephone wires that made us scurry in circles like trapped rats.

Really it was ourselves that we ran from when we ran from each other.

Love had failed me and the world scared me. To the home for the degenerate doomed I returned each night after spilling beer for the rent. Waste begets waste. I would lock the door of my room behind me. The guy in the next room had a giant cross on his wall with manacles attached to the horizontal ends. He was very nice and baked us all muffins, but he didn't drink coffee or alcohol because he said it affected him too much and this made me nervous.

I would open the cracked window and climb out on my little roof. There I would lie in rain and in snow to stare up at the sky and down at the soil. I drew deep breaths and felt my shriveled innards expand. As I mapped the patterns of stars and houses, an inner world emerged, where I could take seeds of past and self and I could sow and grow. Soon I knew the day. I learned to unfurl towards the sun whose rays used to slice painfully into my sleep.

I met a man in black with nine holes pierced in his left ear and one in his left nostril. He wore a chain from his nose to his ear that tears caught in. I took this man to my roof. We planted ourselves there for two years. This made him very happy. This made me very happy. He got bigger and fuller, opening petal by petal with each dawn. He got so big he scared himself. He scared himself so much he ran away.

I go to the café to show off my tattoo of a butterfly. Sometimes pain can birth beauty that lasts as long as flesh. I try very hard to get involved in the conversation but I've lost the refrain and my words chorus inside me, out of tempo and out of tune. The refrain echoes around me but I can no longer sing along:

> *Stay confused by all means, for chaos is freedom, and above all do not feel your feelings, do not name them, do not heal them, show only your scars, your mutilation, your deformity, live only for a slice of life.*

CAMELLIA & JANE

Day finally digs into Camellia's operatic dreams. She writhes away from the paintbrush jabbing into her back. There are horns blaring and wheels screeching and a metallic trill. Noise eats up the last insulating aria, and as she turns the sun chews open her eyes.

The loft is a three-dimensional Pollock painting, colours protruding to trip her on the way to the bathroom. Her putty face wobbles in pain as she slips the contact lenses in and sticks her whole head in a sink full of cold water. Gasping, she rubs her face with a towel as the shocked skin tightens into curvilinear features. She bends to swathe her hair and notices tiger stripes of scabs on her legs. She is dizzy, but when she shrinks to sit three ox kicks pound her fire escape door. The towel slides off her head as she twists into a red flannel nightie. The second she unlocks the door it is pushed towards her, stubbing her big toe. She hops back a bit, then further under the glare of Jane's yellow eyes.

"I've been waiting for you two hours in a diner full of deadbeats, you slattern. What's your damage?"

"Tequila and too much T. Rex. You should be happy I managed to get up at all."

"Fuck you, you trapped me in a cesspool of lukewarm coffee. You owe me big. God, what happened to your legs?"

"Must have been the madcap frolic in the train yard with Chevy Dave. I'd tellya about it but you'd only yell at me." Camellia throws the nightie onto a pyramid of paint tins and untangles a green velvet dress from the blankets on the floor.

Jane snorts into the sharp sweep of her black bob, "Chevy Dave? That's barrel-scraping."

Camellia slips on green lace tights, her long toenails catching and tearing the webs of weeds. Her grey eyes grow mossy and her hair, flapping like soggy nylons on a clothesline, is brushed by rays of day into fine brass chains. Camellia the

Chameleon, coloured by kaleidoscopic life. She slips on black ballet slippers and then straightens to impale her eyes on the angular structure of Jane's face. "I know, I feel stupid. Not just stupid — wormy. Especially about standing you up this morning. I can't rewind and erase it but I'll take you out for lunch, I made good tips last night. The thing is, you know, like last night, it's like I'm in this movie and I'm just a character following some script, and there is me but I don't decide anything. I just be what the movie seems to want me to be. And the screenplay is all improvisational and I don't know whose it is. Yesterday was all kinda like Warhol and last night was all kinda like Lynch — am I being self-aggrandizing? I don't mean it that way. It's just... I don't know... that's the only way I can describe it — and it's always kinda clichéd and in the end very boring. It's like that all the time, this movie thing. That's what is so stupid."

"That is really stupid. If you didn't want to go with Chevy Dave you should have just told him to forget it. People aren't harps in the wind. I'm always myself. I always know what I am doing."

"It's not that I did or didn't want to, it's that I don't know what I want, and what I want doesn't seem to matter anyway. Things happen or they don't, no matter what I do or don't do." Camellia packs her round case haphazardly: crayons, sketchpad, a bubble-blowing kit, a hex-key set, *A Tale of Two Cities*, purple lipstick, a multi-screwdriver, and a deck of tarot cards. She tries to bungy cord it to the back of her old gold bike but it isn't working.

"Here, don't forget your keys or your wallet, either," Jane disentangles the knapsack hanging from a life-size plaster skeleton, "but you have so much fun. You just do things. What do I do? Go to school, study my physics, work in an insurance agency, photocopy autopsy reports. Nobody takes me for frolics in train yards, not with my hatchet-face."

It was true that the architecture of Jane's face was more monumental than luxurious, that her expressions were unyieldingly definite, but this temple to the severity of truth rested on soft curves. Once, in an effort to break open Jane's shell of hard facts so she could wonder with her, Camellia proposed that they paint together. They each had a canvas primed with a black background and planned to paint nude female torsos. Camellia drummed deep peach and bright pink onto the flat black in staccato jags and in minutes a taut torso shook into being, obviously standing straight on her own two feet and flexing biceps in the pose of a bodybuilder, her belly-stretch of womb a glowing jewel. Jane's brush spread generous pats of glistening salmon as if buttering burnt toast. This torso slouched diagonally across the level void, more placid than flaccid, a baroque chaise longue of satin flesh. As Jane's eyes and hands directed the paint in slow sweeps, Camellia studied her certainty and remembered running from her mother's shrieks to rest her head on her friend's shoulder, sobbing into Jane's yielding neck. It was the only time she had seen Jane cry, crying for her.

"Hatchet-face, that's ridiculous. You have a sure face, that's all, not a bland blank page with dimples." Camellia hunches on the packed knapsack and extricates her bike from sharp scrolls of chicken wire. "It's that you're a walking wagging finger, that's the problem. Fuck, where is my fucking wallet? I know I put it somewhere. Want to double to the Gaffer?"

"No, I have to wear this suit to work later. I'll take the streetcar and meet you there." Jane finds the licorice tin filled with Camellia's tips in a doorless fridge. She pushes Camellia over a bit and buckles the tin into the knapsack's outside pocket.

Peddling with the reckless whims of traffic, Camellia feels her porous skin expanding with the humming humidity of the May day, the noxious smog of the revving vehicles, the mingling and clashing odours of dried fish, rotting vegetables and bruised fruit. She swerves to avoid a sharp-eyed pike's head as a group of Portuguese widows flap out of her way and crow at her from the crowded babble of the curb. Her meek smile doesn't placate them as she rides on. In the messy, compressed humanity of Kensington Market, explosions of produce, of tongues, of eccentricities, are contained within a grid of skyscrapers, so that Toronto is still a safely boxed and packaged world. Camellia's heart steps up its rhythm in synchronicity. Saturated, her skin itches inside her. She is a gelatinous Russian doll, the selves of each growth not shed, living on within her, containing each other, layers chafing on layers, each self reaching out for its own dream, phantom arms stretching out like spokes from a wheel whose hub is hidden. Who is she? She contains multitudes. Here, in the Market, she is contained by multitudes. There isn't any space to spill into, the blood blushing the melting fish ice as it spreads trickling down the street.

Jane waits at the cafe. She is concerned about her shoes but otherwise comfortable. She ripples through a German magazine she found in the rack of library discards and anarchist monthlies. The brightly painted Salvation Army furniture and throws of Guatemalan fabric make this place a friend's home. She and Camellia had discovered this café years ago, when they were still underage drinkers. The kitsch had gradually eroded as the posters on the wall were framed, the olive linoleum was replaced with black and white tiles and numerous kitchen appliances were added. Now that there was soft pink lighting they could only afford to come here occasionally.

The first time they'd come here was with their friend Purple Mike, who was still cross-dressing then. They'd just found some old 70s *True Confessions* magazines at the Goodwill Buy-by-the-pound on Queen Street, and they were all giddy with the thrill of being able to buy anything at all. Mike had gotten a mini-skirt too, slipping it on under his dress. He would only wear purple. To celebrate, they'd all dropped half a microdot each and run up to the Market, giggling and spitting and skipping. He'd brought them here and bought a round of coffee. It was probably more the coffee than the acid that made them love their loudness more and more. Taking turns, one of them read the true confessions out loud while the other two mimed the action. When Jane had read out, "He had a long, long face with a towering forehead," Camellia had grabbed her own hairline and chin and stretched them way apart to make a face that catapulted Mike onto the floor and made laughter in all the other customers. Soon the audience had scraped their chairs closer and a couple of older guys even started pulling their faces around too. But when it was Camellia's turn to read, and Jane and Mike had to act the scenes out, Jane had flushed and halted and stayed all Jane.

Revenge weighting her bat-wing brows, Jane scrutinizes the chalkboard menu. Two hours at work equals $18.47 after taxes, her meal should be at least twenty to make up for Camellia standing her up this morning. But no, she did get to read a mystery novel while she was waiting, so ten to fifteen dollars should do it. There is nothing that expensive she wants to eat, they are both vegetarians. She decides to get a fancy drink. She orders Pernod.

As Jane calculates her compensation, a muscular man with tall hair stomps around the tables to crush the foamed bench beside her. Wearing Doc Martens, he kicks the chair opposite so that he can stretch out his legs and rest his boots on it. He takes a pack of contraband Marlboros out of the breast pocket of his plaid shirt with the arms cut off, he throws the pack onto her open magazine. Jane turns her head and narrows her eyes at him, her nostrils flaring. He remains unaffected. This unsettles her for a minute. In a voice that could cut diamonds, she asks, "Where's your invitation, carboy?"

Chevy Dave looks at the magazine, "What are ya, some kinda Nazi?"

"Cam isn't here. I don't know where she is." Jane looks out past the umbrella tables on the sidewalk to make sure that Camellia is, as usual, taking her own sweet giddy time. Out of the corner of her eye, she notices Chevy Dave's tattoo, the skull of a dog with a porkchop hanging from its jaws.

He catches her and flexes his muscle so that the mongrel seems to masticate, "My dog Chopper. Wormfood. Truck ran over him. Hell of a mess."

Lighting a cigarette, he scans the street of bobbing green Mohicans, pink dreadlocks and Gothic vampire manes, "I'm so fucking sick of dye-babies and fucked-up hair."

Jane takes one of his cigarettes, measuring the height of his morass of cowlicks skeptically.

"Dirt," he flips open his Zippo on his thigh, then snaps his finger to spark the flame and light her cigarette, "not hairspray."

Camellia pulls her bike up short in front of the cafe. She can sense Jane's presence inside, and she lifts her nose into the air with indecision. After picturing Jane's confusion if she was on time for once, Camellia decides not to disappoint her.

A textile garden of glowing colours waves at her from further down the street. It is her favourite vintage clothing store, its yard hung with the sequin-dewed remnants of an age when everyone was to be pretty without embarrassment. She is drawn with the avarice of a child approaching a blossoming field.

She locks her bike to the fence and starts spinning a rack, like spinning a wheel of fortune. Who could she be? The right outfit and Diana Prince is Wonder Woman, the Wolf is Grandma, the Prince is a pauper. The problem is, she wants to be everybody. This is called greed.

There is a dress that could twirl her into some vivacity, a vest that could deepen her voice, a pair of bloomers whose powers she can't even imagine. And a crinoline. A stiff, full, purple crinoline with a white stain on the front and a rip in the waistband. There was no mistake, it had been hers once, a handmedown from Mike. He had given her all his clothes after he filled out, became a man, shaved his head and switched to kilts.

The last time she had worn it was that night the summer she was sixteen. The crinoline had made her feel both frothy and hard, something you had to get out of the way for. She had called Jane from the Cruise Motel, giggling, "Guess where I am, guess!" and Jane hadn't been able to guess, so Camellia had handed the phone to one of the guys, who gave Jane directions. It was eleven at night and Jane had to sneak out of the house and take the subway down to Union Station, then take a cab along Lakeshore. This is what Jane saw when she opened the door of the room: a bunch of preppy boys standing in a row with their heads bent and their clean white necks shining like fallen halos. This is what Jane saw when she'd pushed through them: Camellia lying on her back with her eyes closed and her top off and her crinoline arching over her hips and a boy between her legs pulling out of her in surprise and spouting white all over her.

Jane had punched him in the head. The other guys had picked him up and pulled up his pants with Jane screaming at them, "Fucking assholes, get the fuck out, get the fuck out of here."

They had gotten out but they'd left a mess. Jane had started cleaning up the broken bottles, the cigarette butts and Camellia — who still wouldn't wake up. Suddenly Jane had slapped her across the face a few times. This is the part that Camellia remembers. She had coughed and gagged and choked and then puked all over the bed. She was the mess. The whole stinking mess.

Jane had gently led her to the shower and scrubbed her down hard all over. Then she'd balled up all the bedclothes and stuck them in a corner of the room. She'd lain Camellia down, and lain herself down stiff and glaring beside Camellia until Camellia had fallen asleep. She didn't wake up until the next night and then Jane had told her what had happened and what to do about it. Camellia was to go to the rape crisis clinic. Camellia had thought this silly. Camellia had said, "That was just a bad date. If there's a bad date clinic, I'll go." and Jane hadn't spoken to her again all the way back to where Camellia was staying.

Jane had gotten in big trouble for sneaking out and not coming back for two days. Her parents had sent her to live with her grandparents in the States for the whole fall semester of grade eleven. Camellia had yelled at her, "Why are you doing this to me? Just don't go. Just tell them to forget it. What am I going to do without you? Don't you care what'll happen to me?"

Never having had any, Camellia didn't understand rules. Having had too many, she didn't really understand consequences either. She had needed a bad date clinic a lot that fall.

Camellia wads up the crinoline and stuffs it into a garbage can at the curb. Then she takes the vest and bloomers in to pay for them. She enters the dim front room. Before her eyes adjust to the compressed panorama of this treasure chest, she hears her name called by a woman clad in thick crusts of paint. Camellia blinks a few times before recognizing the ex-ex-girlfriend of her ex-ex-ex-ex-boyfriend. "Hey, Cherry."

As Cherry expounds on her loft renovations, gallery shows and upcoming wedding, Camellia is at a loss. The only thing that stands out about her life is that she is never home and her place is a mess. When Cherry asks how she is, Camellia can only say, "The same."

Jane's Pernod arrives. She is not annoyed at its tardiness, but she doesn't know the waitress and Chevy Dave does. This irks her. She swallows the drink in a gunfighter slug and orders a Jack Daniels. Chevy Dave wants a raw steak and a Rebellion. He is only ordering the steak to disgust the waitress and probably all the customers. Jane likes this. In fact, she likes his tattoo, his Zippo tricks, his hatred of hairdos. There is motion in her liver like a coin tossing as she mulls over the magnetic attraction of opposites and the duality of existence inconclusively. He interrupts her contemplation of Heisenberg's *Principle of Uncertainty*. "Everyone is a tofu-sucking veg these days."

Jane is laughing as Camellia swirls around the crowd to run into Chevy Dave's legs barricading her from the chair opposite Jane. Jane notes that somehow on Camellia's journey her costume has accrued a black suede vest and frilly red bloomers. Under the pink lights, Camellia's hair glows orange. Chevy Dave catches her between his shins but she only gazes at him in wisps, directing her widened eyes at Jane. "Sorry I'm late but you'll never believe, I got a job, I mean a real job, I ran into Cherry — remember her? — and she hired me as her assistant teaching the kids art at that place, outdoors even, really it's the best thing, we better spend these tips, they're the last, less money but that's a real job, isn't it?"

Breathless, Camellia drops her knapsack on Chevy Dave's legs and ignores his epithets as she makes it to her seat. His feet now returned to the chair, she digs her bag out from under the table and pulls all manner of recent purchases from it. "I'm celebrating."

As Camellia orders a peppermint tea, Chevy Dave begins to eat the dripping steak with his hands. Jane cackles, watching Chevy Dave try to lasso Camellia with his eyes while she is ripping open packages and knocking things off the table. Something is sinking within Jane, sinking with a spiraling intensity, a whirlpool draining. Camellia with a real job. Camellia ignoring a swain. She is no longer responsible for Camellia, it seems. No longer the restraining arm, the receptacle of confession, the purifying bath of advice, the wagging finger. Her nose wrinkled, Jane washes down the JD. with a stolen swig of Chevy Dave's beer. He doesn't notice the theft, he is upending Camellia's new Godzilla into a glass of water. He asks her, "You coming to the show tonight? We're opening for R.I.P. and you're not working at the bar, right."

Camellia looks straight at him and for the first time he sees her face static, unchanging, and it is not as formless or faithless as it must have been under the flashing neon lights. The green has not faded from her eyes. Suddenly he is slightly afraid of her. There are things in her irises, shapes like leaves, slowly defining themselves, crystallizing, and he can't see himself reflected in her pupils at all. She looks down, pulls her hair from her tea, and says, "No, I have to get up early to start this new job and I want to clean my loft tonight. Maybe clean that fridge I found in the garbage, put its door on so I can have something besides coffee around."

He turns to Jane, "Yeah, what about you? I'll buy you a brew if I see you there."

"A brew? Some hot date." Jane is aware that she is supposed to be at the insurance agency in fifteen minutes and she is not going. She climbs over his lap to go to the phone booth across the street.

"Who said it was a date, what the hell is a date anyway?" Chevy Dave calls after Jane.

"You're not drinking?" he asks Camellia, taking the Chinese medicine balls from her hand and jiggling them, watching her moonish reflection.

"No, I don't feel like it. Drinking is getting boring."

This could be a comment on last night. He says, "What the fuck is that supposed to mean?"

"I've been having a lot of fun but now the fun is changing to something else, that's all."

"In one day?

"That's the way it always works for me. Fast."

Jane returns from the phone gloating, "Hah! I told them I had coryza. It's just the common cold but those fools don't know a taxidermist from a mortician when it comes to multisyllabic words."

Camellia tries to scrunch everything back into the sack, but it must have shrunk in the heat or something. She puts on a leopard-print hat and a belly dancer's belt of chains and coins. This provides enough space to complete her packing. She throws a crumpled ball of bills on the table, "I'm leaving. Hey, Jane, when's your lunch break tomorrow?"

"I finally take a day off to do what I want and you're going?"

"I want to finish my painting before I start working days, get an alarm clock, maybe I should buy some food. You have afternoon classes tomorrow, right? I'll call you at the office in the morning. This art school is near the university, we can eat outside, okay?"

Camellia inadvertently buffets a few coifed heads on her way out. She leans forward as she walks, not because of the weight of her knapsack so much as to strain against the pull of Jane's eyes. Jane is peeved, "What a sniveling wuss."

Chevy Dave spits on the floor but hits his boot. "I'm going over to Sharky's place to pick up some rats and drink his beer. You can come if you want."

Jane smirks and shrugs, draining his Rebellion and wiping her mouth on her white sleeve.

That night Jane looks at her silhouette in the nightclub window and sees that she is haloed with prismatic rays. The thrashing drum beat reverberates inside her ribs, pushing her heart beyond her measured movements of calm surety, the drums punching in and her heart punching out, the limits of her flesh yielding to all motion. Consciously affecting a slight wiggle as she slides out of the booth, Jane stands with her toes pointed together and says in a tinkling voice, "I have to pee."

Chevy Dave lifts his head from the table. For a minute he thinks he hears Camellia. Blurrily, he watches Jane sway to the washroom. The shaking branches of Camellia's graceful limbs seem to be super-imposed onto Jane's solidity. But it is this solidity that holds his glance.

In the acidic light of the bathroom, the mirror distorts Jane's features so that they seem to waver. Jane giggles at this deception, she almost looks like Camellia. She practices her imitation, knowing that Camellia is the key to the locked part of herself that might free itself violently were it not for these exercises. She returns to her seat and looks with scorn at Chevy Dave's form spilled across the table like an overturned bottle. She punches him in the side and he looks up to say, "Hey, you're pretty tough. Not like your flaky friend."

Jane slides over beside him and he drapes his arm off her far shoulder, steadying his head on her neck.

The next morning goes so fast Camellia only has time to get her eyelids unglued. They say on the phone that Jane is still ill. Camellia soaks her greyish, sun-thirsty skin in the artyard and drinks a grapefruit juice for lunch. A mousy girl is colouring on the grass beside her, holding paper under her heel. She has the pudgy, mashed-potato face of kindergarten. Without having met her before, she plays with Camellia's hair. She is eating a tofu wiener, her parents are militant vegans. She stares straight and wide at Camellia and says, "I am a wolfchild. I knowed since I was borned that I am a wolfchild. I eat only meat and nuts. Lots of meat and lots of nuts. I was going to dye my hair blonde last week but my mom said that wolfchilds like their hair the way it is."

Her face stretching with light, Camellia says, "I heard that wolfchilds like to go out and howl at the full moon. Do you do that?"

The girl shakes her head, brandishing a fat purple marker that smells of that aesthetic chemistry called 'grape.' In her mother's voice she says, "No, I watch Cosby and go to bed. Get up, go to school, watch my programs, go to bed. Get up, school, TV, bed. Boring, boring, boring."

Camellia stares at the random violet curves wiggling across the blank page. Sometimes the burden of being is too hard to bear and she settles for seeming. Sometimes believing is as impossible as growing an extra eye between her brows and she settles for seeing with only her myopic two. Sometimes she is only awake when she is asleep and only real in her dreams. She wants to wake up. She wants to shake herself real hard and stretch and wake up, standing on her own two feet.

A patchy sedan stops short at the top of the street, reverses back into the intersection, then drives on past. Jane walks down from the corner in her wrinkled suit. She climbs the fence into the schoolyard, snagging the tail of her shirt. She walks over to Camellia with a pained, squinting expression on her face. She sprawls on the grass with her head in Camellia's lap and says, "I'm such a fucking idiot," then splits her sides with laughter, rocking from side to side.

FALLING

n the music I could lose it. Otherwise it was there all the
time. I couldn't stand watching the pigeons on the roofs
any more. I couldn't stand to see anything fall off the table
or beside the bed, especially not clothes slipping on to the
floor. And I could never catch things, never, not even way back
in gym class. The ashtray would teeter at the edge of the
kitchen table and one of the guys would not think about
elbows and down it would go, the dizziness would swoop me
down between my knees, my fingertips pressing the floor
down a storey. I couldn't fall asleep. I couldn't have anything
to do with any kind of falling at all, ever. Which you can imagine is kind of a liability in this life. So all I did really was wait
for the gigs.

And sometimes it was like everything was falling but me, all
the wires and buildings and streetcars, leaving me alone, suspended, in the same place but suddenly with nothing beneath
my boots, like a hanged man. I'd try to put something under
me again by making the songs pound down in my head, but it
wouldn't work. I needed a Walkman really bad, but as usual I
had no money and no one would lend me one.

It's a distinction we didn't get, I guess, that gave us the
trouble. That line, one of those fine ones, between flying and
falling. All of that running around snorting things and drinking things and climbing the railway tower, swinging from the
pipes in those abandoned factories, and eating Big Mac pic-
nics on top of Bay Street office buildings in our flapping rags,
all of that felt kind of like flying, like getting away with something, like being above it all, like some kind of freedom. Like
when the want ads just take off on you in the park sometimes,
and coast around the air, endlessly amused by the nothing all
around. It all felt like that kind of flying, but now I guess I
know it was a kind of falling, that could only stop with a thud
I didn't hear but felt in my toes somewhere, like a kind of stub

that carried up, getting stronger.

The music worked, as I said. The bass beat could make gravity believable again, and somehow on my side, like it was walking at my side the way you used to, kind of bobbing and flighty but there, bumping into me all the time and crossing my path.

So I knew I had to get a Walkman or I'd keep having this thing about falling and all that, and being this freak about falling, so I just had to get one so I wouldn't see you falling off all the buildings and bridges all the time, and so I did something bad. You know how we had that big rule about not stealing from people but only from big corporations, which are by definition evil unlike people, who are merely stupid? Well I broke it. I was walking by Maple Leaf Gardens and there was a big line of preppies trying to get Depeche Mode tickets, so I sidled up to this girl who reminded me of that girl you went out with — the one who hid you in the closet when her friends came over — and while she was talking to her friend about that date rapist football player we knew in junior high I stole her Walkman out of her purse. So I did something bad.

But so did you, you fuck, you stupid stupid fuck. I don't know. I wasn't there. Maybe it was just an accident because you were so ripped. And maybe it doesn't matter — on purpose or by accident — shit happens, and makes all plans and everything mean fuck all.

Anyway, this Walkman really worked and I listened to it all the time and nobody bugged me about it, because none of them wanted to talk to me anyway. And this one time I was listening to it and walking over the bridge, and our favourite song was playing, not the Motorhead song for doing air guitar but the other one, the Gun Club one about being in love with Ivy from The Cramps, and it was playing and instead of seeing you fall off the bridge I saw you stagediving off the railing and then being carried away by a big crowd of shirtless booted skankers, and I decided that they took you to New York. It was totally fake and cheesy and all, but it worked, so I'm more okay now and every time I think of you I get kind of pissed off about you going to New York and seeing all the good bands, and making up conversations for the pigeons in the window with a Bronx accent, and having fun without me.

EXORCISM

First Layla chisels the pink rosettes off the belly of the chipped white vase. Then she squats on the concrete floor to roll both the belly and the severed neck up in three sheets of *The Globe and Mail*. She fetches her hammer from under the big worktable, untangling it from pliers, wrenches, screwdrivers and a crowbar, and grips the handle loosely. She raises the hammer above her head and brings it down on the largest bulge of print, not too heavily, but enough so that the shape of the package shifts with muffled cracking noises. She does this again and again, each time with a new curve to the downward arc. There is something almost yogic about her movements. The simplest gesture when performed by her seems to contain a hundred steps of miniature motion. But this doesn't mean that she is careful.

In fact, she discovered this method of smashing things quite literally by accident. She needed something to add to the shells imbedded in the clay frame she was making for her Venus painting. It was the middle of the night and the full moon flew in through the warehouse windows to be split on the crack bisecting a mirror propped up behind the kitchen sink. Not wanting to wake Jules, she took the filmy mirror and started to break it with her hands, like breaking bread. The fragmentation went well for a while and she had a small pile of cracker-sized pieces when one new edge sliced into the fleshy mount at the base of her thumb. She went and stuck her hand under cold running water, then wrapped her hand in a greasy tea-towel and applied direct pressure with her other hand. The tea-towel was soon heavy with blood and it dripped a maze around the large studio space as she paced slowly for half an hour. As the wound still hadn't stopped bleeding, she slipped behind the curtain to where Jules was sleeping in bed and took a TTC token out of his jeans' pocket. Then she put on her sanitation engineer uniform and went to the hospital.

It still didn't hurt when it was wiped with alcohol swabs. She was staring in wonder at the pockets of fat webbed with red lines revealed by this gash when the doctor jabbed the local anesthetic needle in and she screamed, surprising herself, since it had been a long time since she'd felt pain. She screamed loudly enough to terrorize the waiting room. She apologized for this as he began to sew her up. By the third stitch the anesthetic had worn off and tears were running down her face as she gnawed on her good hand. The doctor wanted to give her another needle but she refused. The pain of the stitches was half as acute as that of the needle. She could stare at the ceiling and diffuse, erasing the pain and with it herself. When all six stitches were done and her hand was bandaged, she had to go straight to work.

Jules woke to follow the trail of splattered blood. There was no note. He thought about phoning the police, but he was not particularly keen on having them in the studio. There might be some old mushrooms or something stashed around and with his juvenile record he knew they wouldn't be too friendly. He started searching the place himself, emptying milkcrates, knocking over piles of files. He tried to think but he just ended up feeling completely helpless. If he didn't make it to work, he wouldn't be able to cover the rent. He followed the bloodstains out the door and down the stairs and outside to the Ossington bus stop, kitty corner to the warehouse, where they seemed to end. He figured that meant that she'd left of her own volition, so that even if foul play was involved she couldn't be mortally wounded. No one would try to dispose of a body on public transit. As he rode the bus another theory occurred to him. Maybe she just had a particularly heavy period and didn't have any feminine protection. They were all out of toilet paper, that he knew. And all her underwear could be too dirty to wear.

He went to the photocopy shop and asked his boss if she ever got a really bad period and bled profusely. She looked at the bloodstains on his jeans and then phoned the sanitation department to see if Layla had made it to work. She had. She was out on her run. When Jules heard, he wiped his brow, then whistled while he worked.

Layla came into the shop just before his shift ended, and Jules unwrapped her and made fifty photocopies of the black wires crossing the white crescent moon on her mount of Venus for his collection.

She smiles as she thinks about his collection of photocopies and unwraps the vase. Stacks all over the studio and he never even looks at them. They just sit around until they are knocked over and then they acquire coffee rings, spilled ashes and dusty bootprints. She likes this about him. The way he never feels like something has to be done about something. It can just lie there within reach and that is enough.

The vase is not broken enough. She unwraps it and hammers away again, more gently this time, until the pieces are smaller. There is a row of Crown jars on the worktable, lined up against the grimy windows. Each jar contains a different shade of broken pottery. Layla takes the jar of white pieces and pours its contents on to the scratched table surface. She adds the pieces on the newspaper to the pile. Then she turns a desk light on above an intact white teacup and saucer. She stares at the china intently for a long time. While picking at her chapped lips, peeling some of the dry layers off and dropping them on the floor. She takes a square of plywood from a tower of them beside the table, and on its 6" x 6" surface quickly starts arranging and rearranging pure white, bluish white, greyish white, yellowish white, white with a hint of lavender, white with a marine cast, white with a slight blush. The tonal values form an image of the teacup and saucer in mosaic.

What is broken may never be fixed. But it can be used to form a new pattern.

She fills the white jar again and then pours out the jar of red pieces for the background. In the middle of picking out wines, berries, tulips, and pale pomegranate seeds, she lifts her head and tucks her brown hair behind her ear, slightly cocking her head towards the door in anticipation. A bus huffs to a stop outside the window. After a second, striding steps tattoo down the hall. When the scratching at the lock comes, her hair swoops back down on to the table as she bends and continues to wield chips in her tweezer.

Jules opens the door and notices that she is working. He always comes home at the same time, hoping to establish a routine of reacquaintance with her after work, but she is usually involved in a mosaic. He bends down and unlaces his boots, places them softly by the doorway, and eases the door closed. He tiptoes to the fridge and digs some vegetarian chili out of the freezer. He puts it in a pot on the two-burner electric stove that sits on the counter. He sits on a leopard-print pillow on the floor and stares at her awhile, whistling. He gets up and stirs the chili in ten clockwise circles. Then he unearths an old basketball out from under a mound of busted furniture, the perks of Layla's job. He bounces it exactly one hundred times. Then he lets it roll away and serves himself a big bowl of chili. He asks her if she wants any and she says no, she had cheese and crackers and she is full. He is disappointed not to serve her. He eats one bowl, then another, and then takes his third bowl over to her worktable.

He watches her the way city boys watch a bird building a nest.

He edges up on to the far end of the table and swings his legs back and forth, back and forth, watching her put the last pieces into place. His movements rock the table slightly, and so she needs even more intricacy than usual in the motions of her hands. She has not learned the necessity of speaking her needs, like the need for him to stop shaking the table. Such speaking hasn't ever occurred to her, so little does she trust the power of words. Her presence is not so much one of sound as one of space. The space implied, for example, by the shadow of a shaking tree, whispering without speech.

The arrangement finally complete, she sweeps the remaining red pieces off the table and into her jar. She is about to take another piece of plywood and get out the tile glue to transfer the design and make it permanent, when he puts down his bowl, swings off the table and stands behind her, bending as he brushes the hair on the back of her head with the stubble on his chin. She laughs and turns around and rubs her palm along the bristles. And then she looks down into her hands, expecting to see little razor lines of red from his scratchy face, but there are no marks.

"Let's go out," he says, and since they are still at that stage where they must remind themselves of each other's contours and details, he raises her head and looks into her eyes and wonders how they could have so many colours in them that you can't tell if they are green or blue or brown, like some unidentifiable article of clothing bunched up at the side of the road.

"Okay," and she unzips her orange coverall and puts on a floral dress with rips in the armpits, a striped sweater with holes at the elbows, tiger-print tights with fishnets over them, and

Docs. He changes into a fresh white t-shirt and laces his boots on again. They put on their motorcycle jackets and go out.

The Cameron isn't very crowded yet and they slide on to vinyl seats against the wall at a small table in the middle where they can avoid the potential crowding at the bar near the door and the commotion of the band in the back room. They can hear either Axe or Chevy Dave yelling, "Where the fuck are those assholes. Fuck!"

A new waitress comes over and starts hassling Jules about I.D. because he is so short and skinny and his face is so broad and freckled. But she doesn't hassle Layla because Layla's face is so Cubist in its angles, as her nose doesn't quite align with her chin and her eyes aren't completely level, that her small-ness doesn't seem youthful. Neither of them has I.D., but luckily the regular Saturday waitress comes over with Jules' six drafts and Layla's double vodka neat and shot of Kahlua. The uninitiated waitress retreats in shame and Layla allows herself to gloat.

Layla talks as little when they're out as she does at home. This is what first attracted Jules to her, right here in the Cameron, one year ago, while she was finishing high school. They were both here for the Handsome Ned matinee, with its happy hour special of three drafts for $1.65. Happy hour had since been outlawed but Jules, in the privacy of his thoughts, allowed himself the corniness of believing that it was still a happy hour just to be with her here. He is happy to feel the gentleness he perceives in her silence, to sense the seductive complexity behind her lopsided smile, something he accepts without ever hoping to understand. As she accepts him, his need to multiply his connections so that each would remain simple. Except for her.

He likes to talk. Especially about nothing at all. So they come here every Saturday night and Jules talks to whoever happens to be around — the old guy regulars or the band members or people from Layla's high school days — and Layla seems to listen sometimes and other times seems to watch without listening, a dark Cheshire cat.

An old man with a fat red nose lurches across the room to squeeze himself in between Layla and the coifed woman at the next table along the bench. He sets his Blue down on their table and leans across Layla to address Jules. "Did I ever tell you about my brother?"

Layla winces at the booming slur.

Jules says, "Yeah, Pete, the one that died in the war, I know."

Pete says, "You wanna know how he died? I'll tell you how he died. It wasn't like they said in the telegram, that's for damn sure. Let me tell you, I know, I know, I was right there. Run right over by one of our own tanks, that's right. Wasn't even killed by the enemy. You can blame the Krauts for a lot of things but you can't blame them for that, nosirree. Know what the telegram said? It said that he was killed during manoeuvres against the enemy. It's a damn lie! I know, I was there! We was all just joyriding in those tanks that day. Just tearing around the turf. Hell, we even had some dames in some of those tanks, pardon me, Little Sister, Lay, Layla. I'm a gennleman, you know I am."

"Yeah, yeah," Layla says and takes one sip of vodka and one of Kahlua.

"I guess you miss him a lot, eh, Pete?"

"He was a helluva guy, Jules, you can bet on that. I'm the rotten bastard. I'm the rotten bastard and he's goddam dead, goddam goddam dead." Pete starts crying, wiping his nose on his sleeve.

"Hey, Pete, it's okay, buddy, it's okay."

"What kinda rotten bastard."

"Pete, c'mon, it's not like you did anything bad to the guy, right? I mean it's not like you ran him over with the tank."

Layla wonders how Jules could be so sure Pete hadn't run his brother over.

"No, I never run him over."

"So it's okay. You didn't kill him or anything. It's okay."

The regular waitress comes over, "Okay, Pete, time to go, let's go now."

Pete keeps on crying.

"Pete, I don't wanna get Gary to throw you outta here, now, c'mon, you've had enough. Just get home and we'll see you tomorrow."

"What do you have to throw him out for? He's not bothering anybody."

"He's bothering me," says Layla, the almost imperceptible pauses that usually break up her speech, as if another sentence, unspoken, was intruding on the first, becoming more pronounced as she drinks, "Every time. The same fucking thing."

"Jules, he's only gonna to get more drunk and then he's gonna pass out again and then what will I do with him? He has to go out. Now."

"Alright. Let's go, Pete. I'll walk you to the door."

As Jules escorts Pete out, Layla lights a contraband Marlboro and takes more alternate sips of the Kahlua and vodka until they are finished. Then she starts picking at the label on Pete's abandoned bottle of beer. It is starting to get crowded and Jules has to wind his way back through a series of greetings from acquaintances. En route, he bumps into the waitress again and orders another round for him and Layla.

"You know what? We should go stay at my parents' farm this summer, have a vacation," he says, easing back into his seat. "That would be great. Ride the horses. They have eight horses that they rent out by the hour. We wouldn't have to pay."

"I'm not very comfortable, with parents."

"You'd get along with my parents. My mom does water-colours and you could talk to her about painting and my dad can show you how to use a jigsaw."

"I don't like painting any more, it's too wet, and messy. And I know how to use a jigsaw."

"Well, it was just an idea." He starts drumming on the table.

"Let me just think about it. I'd like to go horseback riding. I'd like to get away with you," she butts her nose against his cheek and he stops drumming and he puts his hand on her knee. She doesn't move it away,

They start drinking the next round.

When she puts her empty glass back down, she sees a man standing in front of the table. He is somewhat rotund and his face is puffy around his eyes. Long frizzy grey hair is pony-tailed to punctuate a bald spot, an upside-down exclamation mark. He stares at Layla, intent, an amateur hypnotist.

He speaks with a professionally contrived compassion. "Layla. It's been a long time since we've seen you. How are you?"

Layla keeps her eyes on her glass and lights another ciga-rette. She takes a rapid succession of drags and haloes herself.

"I'm okay."

"Then I'll tell your parents that I've seen you and you're alright." He puts his heavily-ringed hand on her shoulder. She looks at his hand the way she examines vases right before she smashes them, with a studied expressionlessness.

A young Pakistani man in a tuxedo, carrying a basket of roses, cuts in, "Would you like to buy the lady a rose?"

The older man reaches into his Mexican leather bag and hands over some bills, taking a single rose and laying it on the table in front of Layla. She ignores it.

"That's right, I'm all right." Layla looks him straight in the eyes, "So there's nothing more to say."

The man turns around slowly and starts to weave his way out. He looks back at Layla from the doorway as she knew he would, and she gives him a quick blink of her eyes which effectively shoos him out the door.

"Who was that?"

"Just this guy, Bob, whatever."

"A friend of your parents?"

"The leader of Fairfields, the urban commune I grew up in. He ran the school and the philosophy of the whole place, you know, hippy shit, socksucking hippy shit. He's a pompous ass. Can you go get us another round?"

As she waits for Jules to return, Layla thinks about what she usually avoids thinking altogether in order to avoid thinking about. She thinks about Fairfields, and the schoolroom at Fairfields, and her friend Aponi walking slowly out of Bob's office, trailing a pink plastic skipping rope behind her and sucking on the end of one of her yellow braids, and a little Layla watching her, knowing that she herself is next in line for her interpersonal session. She thinks about Bob's hand, how heavy, how thick, on her shoulder, his rings cold against one of her moles as her stomach rustles papers on his desk. She thinks about pain, how she lost it and with it everything else. And she thinks about telling Jules about Bob's hand and everything else about Bob, his breath, the itchiness of the curly hair on his thighs, but she can't hear the words that would tell him this. And she can't see the comfort in such a confession that would both change everything and change nothing at all.

Layla puts out her cigarette and absentmindedly picks up the rose. Gently, she pries the bud from the stalk.

Jules sets down the drinks, "What are you doing?"

"I don't know. Have you ever heard that expression — in the heart of the rose. You know. Look. Where is it?" She examines the pieces before her, squinting like a puzzled schoolgirl, "Is it supposed to be this fuzzy yellow knob on the top of the stem? Or this hole here? Or what?"

He looks into the black hole at the base of the bud, framed by its pucker of petals. "I don't know."

"I don't think there is one. I think it's just an expression." She takes the stem and bud from him and drops them on the floor. "Stupid."

He bends down and picks the bud up, putting it in his pocket.

"Fucking stupid," she says.

He doesn't know what to say to this, so he drinks his draft.

The door opens and Jules falls in. Layla falls in over him. They don't even think about trying to find the light switch. She crawls in the dark to the square of dirty grey carpet in the center of the space. Jules gets half up and stumbles over to a drawer in the kitchen counter. He fumbles with the knob then yanks the whole drawer out. Objects clatter to the floor. He drops down and gropes around until he finds what he is looking for — a candle.

He crawls over to where she is lying spread-eagled and crouches over her to rummage through the zipped pockets on her jacket. He finds her lighter and leans over her to let flames lick the bottom of the candle. Wax drips onto the concrete at the edge of the carpet. He sticks the base of the candle into this pool. It takes him a few fumbles to get it to stand upright. He turns to her, saying, hey, you're all red in this light.

She sighs. He starts taking her jacket off and his. She runs her hand slowly up under his t-shirt and circles his left nipple with the nail on her right index finger. He takes his t-shirt off. And her sweater. It gets caught around her head and he kisses her mouth through it, feeling tufts of wool scratch his tongue. He gets it off.

He goes to work unlacing their boots. He keeps getting them more knotted up. She pulls her hair together on top of her head, twisting it into a unicorn horn. He pulls her boots off and then his. She arches her back and raises her hips, still holding the unicorn horn, so he can reach under her and start peeling off her tights and underwear. He takes this opportunity to kiss her vagina lightly and she jerks her bum back down, letting go of her horn. When her tights are off, he stands up to take his jeans off, but he starts to fall over when they bunch at his thighs and he lets himself fall beside her.

She rolls onto her side and tries tugging one leg off, but it doesn't work, so she sits up, swaying, and straddles his ankles, reaching behind her to tug his socks off by the toes. She falls on to her back and pulls his jeans towards her by their cuffs. He points his toes a bit so they won't snag on his ankles. She sits up again and unfolds her dress over her head. She balls it up and puts it under her neck as a pillow. He disentangles his legs from her and fumbles for his jeans, and takes a condom out of one of its pockets and opens the package with his teeth and, kneeling between her legs, tries unsuccessfully to put the condom on. She leans forward and helps him, rolling it down between her thumb and index finger as he holds the tip, and she lies back down as he moves over her to kiss her lips.

She avoids his open mouth, peppering his face with little butterfly kisses and tracing his lips with her nail. He tries to move back down her body, letting his lips take each step, but she doesn't let him, she holds his chin up by her face and squeezes his erection between her thighs. With her left hand cupping his scratchy chin and her left thumb in his mouth, she moves her right hand down and opens her thighs and begins to insert him. It is hard, trying to get him in, but he helps her by shoving a bit although he is confused, she is so dry, her vagina is so dry, it feels like it's going to squeak, she and he are going to squeak, and why would she want him in so soon? He doesn't know but he tries to please her, rocking back and forth a couple of times to pull the moisture down, but it doesn't flow down, she is still dry, dry as a bone, dry as a desert, and it hurts him and it must be hurting her, and he starts to feel a bit sick, he feels like he is raping her and it makes him feel a bit sick, and he holds the condom at the base and pulls wrenchingly out of her because she is still so squeakingly tight around him, and he pulls out and tries to kiss her vagina again but she flips onto her stomach. She flips over and pulls her knees up underneath her and twists her head and shoulders around so that her outstretched arm can reach him and her finger can again encircle his penis, but this time she moves it towards her anus, she is butting the bulb of his penis against the rosette of her anus and now he is really confused.

He had had that exploration with her the first night they were together, where he started to do things with her, asking do you like this? do you like this? and she would nod or shake her head, and when he had kissed her vagina she had nodded, and when he had pressed his finger at the pucker of her anus she had shaken her head firmly, and when he told her it was her turn he had also shaken his head when she circled his anus with her fingernail. He had had a girlfriend who had nodded about this, and he didn't mind if she liked it and he would do it then and not feel any shame or anything, but he never liked it much himself, although he didn't tell her. But to Layla he had said that's where pooh comes out! with an air of faux innocence that instantly charmed and they had laughed. And now she is trying to work him in there, and he doesn't understand, and he asks her what she is doing but she says to just shove it in, hard, and he has never heard her talk this way but he wants to please her, he makes himself shove it in, and she is sobbing with her face pressed into her dress and her back at a downward slope from him, and her back is all red from the candlelight and white from the impressions on the carpet, it is like an open wound like pockets of exposed fat with blood webbing them in fine lines, and she is crying with her fist tangled in her hair and he feels sick, like he is raping her, and it is hurting him, burning his skin, and he can't do this. He pulls the pulp of his penis out of her, almost twisting it out, unscrewing it and he yanks the condom off, this hurts, and throws it across the room and throws himself down beside her and as he lands tears unwillingly slop out of his eyes and he says he can't.

She doesn't respond. She is busy with her exorcism, her catharsis. She is in the grip of a familiar old pain. A pain that fills her fully so that she doesn't feel empty any more. A pain that shows her how to feel at all again. A new pain, that she is bringing upon herself, that isn't being forced upon her, that ultimately might erase the old pain and free her to feel unfamiliar pains and all kinds of things besides pain. And she eases off crying, feeling vaguely proud of herself, starting to fall asleep, more like starting to pass out, and she reaches beside her to pat him heavily on his chest right where his heart nests and she says it's okay, it's good, you're not some fucking asshole, fucking assholes, and she slurs into sleep leaving her hand over his heart and leaving him there in the hole inside of her and crying drunk and sleepy and thinking about what she has told him. She has told him something. What exactly she has told him he doesn't know, and maybe he doesn't need to know exactly.

He doesn't sleep. He blows out the candle and lies in the dark watching the pale light of winter dawn spread unthinkingly across the ceiling, catching on pipes, and he realizes that the light is a fainter grey than smoke, a grey that is light without really illuminating anything, and finally he closes his eyes.

When he wakes again the ceiling is a darker grey and he knows that it is dusk. She has rested her head on his chest and embraced him in her sleep. She begins to stir, and rolls over on her back and throws her arm across her eyes and gasps, "My head feels like reconstituted shit."

He kisses her elbow and gets up. He puts on his jeans and shuffles in his bare feet across the dusty cement floor to the old claw-foot tub beside the fridge. He starts to fill it. He picks up the contents of the spilled drawer and puts them away. He takes a couple of candles and places them in the wrought-iron holders hanging on the wall above the bath and lights them. He pokes his finger into the tub to test the water and then turns the faucets off. He turns to her lying on the floor, but then turns back to the tub and pulls the rosebud out of his pocket and starts to scatter the petals on the surface of the water. Even though they have darkened and hardened into jagged edges, they are still mostly soft. He crushes one between his fingers and sticks it on his nose, inhaling to keep it in position (it smells good) and then he turns to her and says, "Have I told you" (the petal falling as he speaks) "about my brother?"

She laughs and then winces, her hands functioning as vises for her forehead. He pulls her up and picks her up and carries her over to the bath. He tries to lean down to place her in it gently, but she is too heavy, and he stumbles, and she splashes in. She sinks right under for a few seconds, then sits up abruptly, laughing, petals sticking to her chest like so many scabs. She leans over to kiss him and, with her great muscular strength earned by hoisting old sofas into dump trucks, she pulls him down into the tub with her, breaking the surface of the water again, letting the bath slosh and spread across the floor.

And it's alright. Everything is all right because now she knows he is safe, and now he is kind of new and she is kind of new too.

Even in the thumbcurled hush of the hour before downtown's businesslike dawn, the house seems capable of a careless and unceasing cacophony. While all of the other houses on the street are muzaked with improvements — three-story Victorian row houses stripped of gingerbread and sporting new concrete and wrought iron porches, paved-over front lawns, brown-framed screen windows — this house is a revel of ruin. Seatless chairs, stained futons, milkcrates full of polka records and headless baby dolls, rusty bicycle frames, mouldy *papier maché* sculptures of big-eyed aliens, three-legged tables, rolls of chicken wire and gutted bags of kitchen refuse bulge out the wooden railings of the front porch and fill the bank-card-size yard. On the roof of the porch toy trolls are strewn, and two mannequin legs protrude from the open window of a second floor bedroom. The feet are useful for troll retrieval.

This is what convinced May to rent the room — not the trolls but the screenless windows that allowed parts of the body to reach outside. That and the fact that the room for rent looked out over a tarpaper roof to the forgotten backyard. There wasn't anything else she could afford with her telemarketing wages really.

What confuses her is why they had rented the room to her. Or rather why Petra had, as May didn't meet the rest of the household until a series of random hallway collisions flattened her against the walls all last week, her first week in the house. She had dressed her best to go apartment hunting, in her white blouse with the lacy collar and her freshly dry-cleaned navy-blue slacks. She had even worn nylons. And she had looked shyly at Petra's laddered black tights under cut-off shorts and layers of holey t-shirts, at Petra's eyes outlined in black swoops that met at her temples, at Petra's jangling chains safety-pinned in a tangle about her hips, as Petra had stared at her, open-mouthed and wide-eyed, had stared at her, May, as if May was one of the talking trees from H. R. Puffnstuff. And May wonders why she had continued to ask Petra questions about the rent, the housemates, and the yard, when Petra had only answered with a laugh-shrug-headshake-laugh reply each time. But mostly, May wonders why Petra wound up saying, "Whatever. The rent is $200 plus. I don't care what you do with the backyard. Give me first and last and you can move in anytime."

Mostly, May wonders why she is here.

Why, why, why, why, why.... She bangs her feet against the footboard of her grandmother's sturdy single bed until the whys and the bangs drown out her stupid wondering.

She stops kicking her heels as dawn brings her housemates straggling in from their various nocturnal activities. Her room is next to the bathroom and a large old vent with an elaborate brass screen makes a hole between the two rooms. She can see an edge of light, and always expects to see feet but never does. She can hear everything that goes on in there.

First Suzy comes in and pees haltingly and doesn't flush. While she is mildly cursing to herself — probably combing out tangles — Petra runs up the stairs and pounds on the door. "Fuck! Let me in! Fuck! Please! Goddam it! NOW!"

May knows that Petra has left the front door wide open again. Suzy creaks the bathroom door open and Petra rushes past her to puke great gushes of liquid into the toilet, gasping, "Fuck! Fuck!" everytime the mixture of her vomit and Suzy's pee splashes back into her face. May can hear Suzy's Birkenstocks shift weight in the doorway. As Petra's puking subsides, Suzy sighs and says, "You know, maybe if you didn't stick your finger down your throat after every little bit of crap you actually ingest, you wouldn't throw up every time you get drunk. Or maybe you should switch to pot, it might mellow you out."

"Mellow?" Petra spits in the sink. "Just fuck off with that granola shit, wouldja, I don't want to be some fat Deadhead shit, okay."

"You're such a bitch, fuck." Suzy stomps down the hall and slams the door. Crosby, Stills and Nash play from her room.

"CSN, now I'm really going to puke." Petra runs some water and then her footsteps go past May's door to her own. Soon, TSOL is playing in the house too.

May hasn't heard any brushing of teeth so far. She worries about this vaguely. It's not like any of them have dental plans. She had put her Waterpik in the bathroom and left a note authorizing its use by the household, assigning different nozzleheads to each, but no-one seems to use it.

In the lull between arrivals May dresses quietly, easing open the squeaky drawers of her old dresser. She has to remember to rub them with some soap. She puts on her old jeans and reaches into their back pocket, pulling out a tattered and many-times-folded piece of paper. She sits down on the bed and spreads the paper out over her quilt, looking out the window into the fuzzy and permeable grey light.

On the paper is a smeared map. Although the graphite of the pencil lines has blurred, it is still obvious that this was neatly, even painstakingly, drawn. This is a map of her grandmother's vegetable garden, and May is going to recreate the garden, in small scale, to honour the recently deceased woman who had loved her neatly and painstakingly. She is going to use the backyard. She had consulted the other members of the household for permission during hallway encounters, and they had said they didn't care. Which was what she suspected they would say, since it seems to be their answer for everything.

May pulls a box out of the closet as the front door slams shut. Two sets of reeling feet careen up the stairs to the top. Two giddy bodies collapse on each other in giggles and two

voices scramble shrieking into the bathroom. The shower
shoots on, there are unzipping noises, soft thuds of clothes hitting the linoleum, then a tussle of plastic as shower curtains are
opened, tucked into the clawfoot tub and closed. In no time
at all, May hears wet slap, pound, wet slap, pound, and Poppy's
pained whimpers as Frank sodomizes her in the shower again.
May finds herself wincing in time with Poppy's squeaks. She
doesn't sound like she is having a good time, but what does
May know? And what can she do about it anyway.

Frank says, "Babybabybabybabybabybabyohhhhhh.baby-
babybabybaby...."

Knowing that they will be a while, May opens her door
and takes this opportunity to slip out unnoticed. If she
thought about it, her housemates would intimidate her altogether. They can not be known as she knows how to know
people. They so nonchalantly live things May doesn't even
want to know about.

In the kitchen May finds Mondo staring in the freezer of
the fridge. It is solid ice. He is holding a tub of ice cream and
staring at the ice taking up all the room in the freezer. He
turns to May, "You got to help me eat this shit. It's fucked."

"Sorry, I can't eat that for breakfast. Thank you anyway,
though."

With Mondo in the kitchen, and Frank and Poppy's ferrets
in the dining room, and that band sleeping in the living room,
there is nowhere to go downstairs. May puts on her lumber
jacket and goes out through the back shack, with Mondo
yelling, "I hate Mondays," to himself.

She takes her box to the aluminum shed recently deposit-
ed beside the shack. This is her inheritance, the garden shed
and all it contains: shovels and trowels and hoes and her grandmother's gardening gloves, which are too small for May. Since
the oily work gloves she has borrowed from her housemate

Axe are far too big, May decides to forgo gloves and let this ritual mark her hands as she hopes it will mark all of her.

She puts the seeds and the map in the shed. She hauls out a spade and starts digging up the weeds, throwing their brittle and obnoxious long bodies into a pile after shaking clinging earth off their roots. There is one nest of fossilized Queen Anne's Lace (or fennel, she can't tell the difference) that has sprouted atop a hillock in the middle of the yard. It is as tangled and bushy and matted as May's lately neglected brown hair. And its roots are as black as hers. She hacks away at this clump with pruning shears. Then she starts to dig up the hillock to get the roots out and level the site for a tidy garden to feel at home here.

She slows down a bit. The city has speeded her up, taught her impatience, a certain greed for time. She misses how gradually time passed back in Wellington. How she pitied the kids on TV because something happened to them every week. How reading seemed so fast to her. How slowly her grandmother moved when dusting the Royal Doulton figurines on the mantelpiece, or washing a casserole dish of its tuna, or putting her hands over May's to teach a purl stitch. Mostly, May misses her grandmother, Amaryllis. So named because May's great-grandparents thought it would keep her out of trouble to have a name that would be memorable when bandied about. And the name had kept Amaryllis out of trouble, which is probably why May's mother had got into it. And stayed in it, no doubt, wherever she is.

Just like that the day has moved into afternoon and Axe's band starts practicing in the basement, where he also sleeps. It sounds like the band staying in the living room has joined them. It sounds like maybe a horde of antagonistic forces has congregated to wreck havoc on the hearing-unimpaired of Toronto and vicinity. As much as May misses slowness, she also

misses quiet. And cleanliness. At her grandmother's place, even
the soil seemed clean, in a way nothing can be in the city.

Here, the soil is greyish and hangs together in little balls at
the top layer. Then it gets thicker and becomes a cakey clay. It
is at this deeper layer that May's spade strikes a hard plane and
sounds a hollow protest.

May wrinkles her forehead in perplexity. Perspiration flicks
itself from the furrows plowed in the tight freckled landscape of
her brow, where no warm hand smoothes itself in mutual comfort anymore. She takes a deep breath and starts digging again,
her muscles stretching and contracting, tiring and persevering,
presumably grimly whipped on by strands of pioneer DNA.

She has unearthed something. It is a carved wooden box,
grey like the soil, rotten with a rusty hasp guarded by an even
rustier little lock. The lock eyes May with the vulnerable suspi-
cion of a baby turtle in its shell. She pants in its face. She catches her breath, swings her breath back out again, and waits for
her breath to return to her at a more measured pace. Then she
sets the box on the ground and her raw red hands grip the
smooth handle of a metal claw, the varnish on the wooden handle worn away where her grandmother had held it so often.

May stands there, looking down. Wielding the claw as if
prepared to attack or defend. Then she bends down and gently traces the barely discernible and dirt-encrusted carvings on
the box with the claw. Swirls and swallows. She doesn't expect
to find anything really. Some child's dead hamster or collection of marbles. Nothing that will speak to her or lead her anywhere. Just an "Oh look what I found buried in the yard,
hmmm" kind of thing. After all, it was she who had gone
through her grandmother's things, packing what no-one could
use — hairpins, Christmas tree ornaments, new packages of
Depends, small black lace brassieres — into garbage bags for
Goodwill. It had taught her that the detritus we leave behind

us seldom carries our messages once we are no longer there to interpret them. With a shrug she pries the box open.

Inside the tattered red velvet jewelry casing, resting on the raised walls of the sectioning compartments, is a pickle jar. Bick's. With a cartoon pickle, obscenely green and happy, waving and winking at her. The graphics look mid-Sixties, hip and self-important. Floating inside the jar, in some morbid and medical equivalent to amniotic fluid, is a tiny human foetus, black eyes minuscule beads, curled paws clawlike against its caved-in chest. It is vaguely pink and wormlike, a plump little artifact suspended in a cloud like a thoughtless sea creature caught in a tidepool.

This find gives May pause. The drama of it suggests some kind of significance. She searches among all available interpretations. It just isn't fitting, as her grandmother would say. She had started digging to carry on her grandmother's legacy. A legacy that consists mostly of the ability to grow things, but that also includes other qualities — honour, dignity, integrity, compassion, gentility — that have gotten all tangled up in the garden for May, because that is where she always pictures her grandmother, and those are the qualities her grandmother embodied, without instruction but within every deed. Amaryllis would be working in the garden while May sat beside her reading *Alice in Wonderland* or *Winnie the Pooh* or whatever, sensing the Eden that Amaryllis was growing in her. May had started digging to manufacture some kind of sign for herself that her Eden still existed. And would thrive. It would have been apt if this artifact was a chest filled with gold coins like those left for Pippi Longstocking by her cannibal king father. Or a bundle of love letters such as Nancy Drew might have found. Some nourishment of words or currency that would bloom a future before her, a future of generosity, of safety, and of love. What kind of omen was this?

Her garden would not grow and she would not be good. She would isolate herself in her doubt like all of her house-mates. She would continue to find excuses for nihilism lurking in her morning coffee cup and in the shadows of buildings looming over her purposeful passages through the city to work every afternoon. When she met a man or woman that her loins called to, she would not find anything on the other side of the bed but a dusty mirror, a distorted echo of her own songs of emptiness. It was a lie, her legacy. She could not make anything grow herself.

The screen door bangs behind her and she turns to see the smallness of Petra nimble on towards her, her black spikes of hair stalwart in the swift spring breeze. Petra bends over May's hunched form and peers into the box.

"Holy fuck!" she says, "Is that ever cool! We got to put that on the mantelpiece in the living room. That is so fucking cool!"

May looks up at Petra. This is what her grandmother, a P.G. Wodehouse fan, would have called 'wonky'. How could she have forgotten that, Amaryllis sighing and giggling at the same time over a tomato with a growth resembling an erect clitoris, or a zucchini that wore the face of a prime minister, Amaryllis saying, with an irrepressible and sly glee, "Life is just all-round wonky sometimes, that's what it is."

May allows Petra to bear the jar into the house aloft on Egyptian hands over her head and call the others. Suzy, Frank, Poppy, Mondo, and Axe gather round and exclaim, a chorus of "Fucking cool!" May feels something stirring in the house. It is the first time they have all been in the same room together at once, it is spring, it is a discovery that they all find new at the same time. It is something unbidden and without reason, and maybe without a chance to last, but it is good and feels like hands clasping, like Cindy Lou and the Whos in Whoville all swaying in a circle and singing their Whoville song.

**CONFOUNDING
THE HOUNDS**

It took a lot of flattery before I realized I was prey. Frankly I liked it for a while, the attention — really, the admiration. Liked the heads turning in restaurants, the cars slowing to honk and beckon, the way their eyes would go all wonder like in the presence of something holy and beyond themselves. I would wear these costumes from Kensington Market: satin evening dresses from the '30s, black cocktail dresses from the '40s, everything rhinestone and satin and feathers. Writing exams with shoulder length gold lamé gloves on, my arms flashing all Gilda Glinda good witchy under the high school's fluorescent lights. Like I could make magic just by being, just through adornment and adoration. I glided around with an anachronistic poise and felt stars twinkling around my head like Marquez butterflies, and it was like I was truly blessed. Every day a parade and I a princess, Rita Hayworth, Grace Kelly, Audrey Hepburn.

The first thing that spoiled it was the way the eyes would fix and glaze somewhere on me when I talked. I felt them pasting on to me. I walked around with all these eyeballs pasted on me, Girl Scout badges or skateboard decals plastering me over. Then it was the hands too, I was always squeezing through a thicket, my hair and skirt and breasts catching on all of them and having to disentangle myself and this causing trouble.

Then it was the please — no — yes — no — please — no — what-do-you-mean-no arguments all the time, and the way they'd take my hand like it was an empty glove they owned and use it to rub on themselves. The off-on-off-on-off-on argument, and all the swatting, and how very careful I had to be not to hurt feelings, and how mad they could get if I did not appreciate their attention, which was getting harder and harder to do.

The guidance counsellor kept giving me mandatory appointments, and he'd meet me at the door of his office smelling of lemon drops and pepperoni, and put his hand on my hip and escort me to this low chair. He'd sit me down in the chair and stand in front of me, his crotch at my eye level and growing, and ask me if I had a lot of boyfriends and didn't I find high school boys too immature since I was such a smart girl, and didn't I know I was heading for trouble, and the whole time he talked I'd be seeing him grow bigger, so much bigger than me.

I did seem to need some kind of guidance. There was my old friend from junior high who decided that our going to the movies like we'd done a thousand times before was suddenly a date. Even though I took the precaution of sitting in the very first row. Even though I wore my old jeans. And I had to flick his hands off me over and over, until finally I attempted a clearer message by standing up and dumping our popcorn on his head with everyone yelling at me for blocking the screen. The next night I found him overdosing in the bathroom at this party and he'd written on the mirror: "Dump popcorn on my corpse, you bitch. You broke my heart."

I took it pretty hard. Everyone did. We stayed all night in the hospital and then visited every day as he recovered. He would have to be on meds for his heart the rest of his life, the doctors said. He had a bad heart now. He would order us around, make us buzz and dye his hair, sew patches on his army pants, go get him a falafel or some mangos. Then once when he and I were alone he ordered me to sleep with him. He said he'd really kill himself if I didn't. So I did. Worrying about a nurse or tech coming in. Wondering if a bad heart might be catching. Hoping the exercise would kill him in a perfect crime kind of way.

There was also this guy that lived down the street with his wife. He was some kind of photographer, he said. He would drive his car slow beside me as I walked to the subway. All I could see was his asymmetrical blonde haircut sweeping back and forth over his eye. He'd say, "Why don't you come over to my studio after school? I'll show you my pictures of my wife." I went once because he offered martinis and I'd never had a martini before. He showed me all these pictures of his wife, who was Korean and naked, and he talked about how beautiful she was. I agreed. Then I got really sleepy from the martinis, and when I woke up in his wife's bed I was naked and a flash was going off in my face. He said he'd send the pictures to my mom if I didn't sleep with him and I said to go right ahead. My mom hung them in the hallway. Apparently he had the kind of fame that encouraged forgiveness.

Walking home from school became a manoeuvre, demanding dekes and route changes and eyes in the back of my head. There was the photographer guy in his car, and then sometimes boys following me from school, and then there was this guy who went to a nearby private school who I never want to run into again. I was going home one day and saw him walking on the railroad tracks parallel to my sidewalk. The reason that I looked over was that he was reciting that monologue about Juliet and the envious moon loudly, all Barrymore and Olivier. It made me happy to think that later that night I would sum up the day and be able to say, "Today when I was walking home there was a guy wearing a tie and doing Shakespeare on the tracks all Barrymore and Olivier." It made me happy to think there was a kind of person in the world who would be walking home from school along the tracks and would feel all that Shakespeare inside, all shiny, and would just have to let it out right then and there. It made me kind of happy, and I started doing the part about the vestal liveries all sick and green and none but fools do wear them, and then he noticed me there and climbed the fence to ask me my name. I told him.

An introduction is not the same as an invitation but I guess he was confused, since he pushed me against a telephone pole and shoved his long tongue in my mouth and started writhing against me. He was a tall, spidery boy. I almost laughed, it seemed so absurd, and then I wanted to yell. It was broad daylight and the woman I baby-sat for walked by looking at me funny, but I couldn't yell with his tongue down my throat and all my squirming to get away must have looked like some kind of passion. I pretended I was just part of the telephone pole. He came in his pants against me and then ran away really fast, leaving me on the sidewalk all dazed, and wishing I was just a telephone pole.

It just seemed to pervade. The boys at school, men in cars, men on the sidewalks, teachers at school, friends of my parents, and that's when I knew I was prey, that that's what it means to be prized, and I didn't want to have anything to do with it at all any more. I just wanted to peel them all off me, stretch my cramped limbs out, turn all eyes away and fade back into myself, safe.

The night before I did it I saw this boy from school standing across the street from my window again under the streetlight, looking up. He was there for hours, smoking, but instead of this being a thing of pride or sweetness it just made me mad. He wasn't waiting for me, not me, not even the person I seemed to be. I don't know what he was waiting for, but I started to hate it, this thing he was waiting for that didn't exist but seemed to be using me as its substitute or reasonable facsimile. That's when I got the notion of tricking it, of fooling them all.

The next day I skipped school to go dumpster diving. I found a huge pair of men's work pants, a big white shirt with sweatstains in the armpits, and an enormous plaid suit jacket in hangover hues. I bought a pair of Wellingtons at the Salvation Army and practiced stomping all the way home. My best friend Mike came over and cut all my hair off with his Swiss Army knife, and dyed it grey. Then we went over to Jane's house and she taught me how to spit without dribbling on myself.

I was feeling really good. I was knocking all those ballet lessons out of me and slouching and sitting with my legs spread and resting my boots on things and using all those big loose gestures boys have that are like planting flagpoles all around them. I was picking my nose and scratching my belly and burping with vigour, and letting my body be a giant middle finger raised in rudeness.

The hardest thing to learn, but the one that stuck forever, was clumsiness. Bumping into things, dropping things, stepping on things. This training took maybe a month, and then I was all settled in to this free new skin, all stompy and loose and to hell with it.

But there was still one persistent guy who kept asking me out. I kept saying no. I skipped our English class one day because I was on a roll in the rummy game at the local coffee shop, and after the class was over Camellia came in full of what I'd missed. She said that everyone just talked about me all class, because Mr. Ramsey was asking about the change in me lately and Bill, the persistent guy, said, "Did you see her boots? It's obvious she's extremely sexually repressed," and the class had wondered and argued about this for a while before Mr. Ramsey steered the discussion back to the deterioration of my attendance record. When Camellia told me this it was like I was wearing a cap and gown and she was moving the tassel from one side to the other across my face, and I knew that forever after this the pesty things flying about my head would be only my own ideas, and maybe some mosquitoes in the summer, and it felt really good to be rid of all those stars, to sprawl starless and bold and tricky, taking up way more space.

SELENA & BOBBY

mpatient, Selena waves her red hands in front of her, as if this action can shoo away the snowflakes settling on her thick white pancake make-up. She stops in the alley and puts down her round, stickered suitcase on a high snow bank. She clicks the case open and rummages around red sequins and tape cases until she finds a gold compact. She opens it. Snow falls on her belongings. A black-ringed green eye stares back at her. The mirror is too tiny. She pads more white powder across her face by touch. Then she lightly feathers her fingertips down her narrow nose to sweep off the excess. She presses her cheeks in to dig for bones. She runs her index finger under each deep-set eye to stem the smear of eyeliner. She packs up and continues down the alley, kicking her knee-high granny boots against the basement entrance to a ware-house to shake off clumps of snow. She has to put the suitcase down again to open the big metal door with both hands. She stumbles down the concrete steps and opens the second door.

"Hey, Frankenstein."

"Hey."

The leering man angles his lurch away from the doorway so that she can pass. She affects a cool blind stare, sucking in her cheeks and lowering her eyelids, as she weaves through the crowded tables. She prefers this runway to the one at work. There, the eyes shrink her, erase her, while magnifying her flesh so that what jiggling femaleness she has left becomes a white flag of surrender, billowing on the stage in prescribed gyrations, parodying the primal in a fluid mechanics of display that makes her disgusted with herself for conjuring desire in those she despises. Here, the eyes expand her, gild her, bless her. She becomes so much more than herself, conquering their self-absorbed indifference, seizing from them some recognition. Here she is somebody, not just a body. She can hear whispers as she passes tables, conversations interrupted by her presence, which must be remarked upon. She approaches a table in the corner, dumps her suitcase on the butt-strewn concrete floor, and opens it, her every gesture a commanding flourish.

"Who wants to buy a brand-new Walkman?" she says, holding the tape player up in front of her, "Still in its package."

A woman in overalls with a shaved head says, "I'll let you have two drinks on the house for it."

"Fuck off, Tanya. This isn't some piece of shit, it's a forty dollar Walkman."

"Okay, three drinks. Otherwise, I could just five-finger it myself."

Tanya gets up to go get the drinks and Selena takes her seat beside Bobby. He puts his hand on her arm and leans toward her. He raises one black chevron eyebrow. She bites the end of his broken nose lightly. "How was dish-pigging?"

He puts on a rasta accent, "How you feelin'? Feelin' hot, hot, hot." He sneers, revealing a missing tooth. "If I have to hear that fucking song one more time, I'm going to take up a new career as a serial killer. How was strip-pigging?"

"I got fired. That's why I sold the Walkman. It was supposed to be a present for you."

"I told you, you can't get away with being late every day."

"Oh, don't worry, I'll buy you a bezillion Walkmans when my trust fund comes in. Besides, that wasn't it, you asshole. Some fat prick in the audience yelled out *Get that Ethiopian off the stage!* during my show." She bellows the comment out so that heads turn, and then she bursts into laughter with the rest of her and Bobby's table. The boys had been watching her silently since she'd arrived.

"Well you are a bone machine," says Axe, across from Bobby. "I still got bruises on my hips."

She kicks him hard under the table as Bobby climbs over

her to go to the washroom.

"Very witty repartee, fuckhead," she glares at Axe.

He shrugs, staring at her. "What's the big deal? He knows anyway."

"Doesn't mean you have to brag about it. I only told him because you're the fucking Chlamydia King, and so we had to go to the clinic again because of you, fuck."

"No, you told him because you couldn't resist the attention." Selena spits at him. "Fuck you. And your STD too."

Axe dips his finger into the spittle on the table in front of him and licks it. "No, I'll fuck you. Any time."

"You fucking wish. You fucking wish I'd be that wasted again." She smiles like the snake that ate the cat that ate the canary.

Axe takes a long swig on his beer, his bleached blonde dreadlocks flipping back to reveal his sly, flushed face. Beside him, Chevy Dave tips his chair back and tilts his head to roll his eyes up to the ceiling. His spikes of dirty brown hair point at the table behind him where Frannie and Poppy are sitting. Laughing and poking each other, they snap their fingers on his head until he bends forward again. Tanya comes back with the drinks, "Three Selena Roses. Now give me my Walkman."

Selena lines up the pink drinks in front of her, cranberry juice and tequila. She slides the Walkman across the table to Tanya. "Hey, Tanya, how about letting us play here some night?"

"I don't think so. Not after last time."

"Aw, come on. If you had a bigger pit, there wouldn't have been a problem."

"Yeah, if I had a bigger pit then there wouldn't be as many tables and then there wouldn't be as many people buying drinks."

Tanya slouches off as Bobby comes back to claim his seat. "Hey, Selena, let me have one of those Pink Vomits, wouldja?"

"It's not Selena, it's Roz, and you're not Bobby, you're Boz. I decided at work today."

Axe says, "That's fucking cheesy."

Selena says, "That's the whole fucking point. Roz from Rose, Boz from Bobby. How white-trash can you get? We'll have a christening party at a gig with a buffet. Velveeta, Spam, Kraft marshmallow and jello salad, pork rinds...."

"What, and then change the name of the band to Roz and Boz? No way. No fucking stars. It's The Chlamydia Club, equal billing," Chevy Dave speaks for the first time, having been busy practicing lip gyrations along with the GenX that is playing.

"Fuck, Chevy Dave, you never want to do anything." Selena elbows Bobby.

"I'm not going to be called Boz. This whole cult of white trash culture is fucking insulting."

"Oh, are we going to whine about your childhood again?" Selena pouts.

Bobby finishes one of her drinks. "No. Don't be such a bitch."

She drains her last drink and starts burning holes in the plastic cup with her cigarette. There is silence at the table. Axe and Chevy Dave lean back and watch her. She rests her head on Bobby's shoulder and looks up at him with wide eyes. "Sorry."

Bobby nods, "Whatever."

Axe and Chevy Dave look at each other. As Selena starts licking Bobby's face, they put on their motorcycle jackets and plaid scarves. Chevy Dave rouses his German shepherd from under the table. They leave without a word.

Selena gets up from the table and starts to dance to the Nina Hagen song that is playing. She moves her thin white limbs in slow serpentine spirals, a new constellation forming, exploring space to find its place in the darkness. She is the star he wishes upon again. She flashes a five-pointed hand on to his, trying to get him to rise and join her, but he shakes his head and pulls her in instead, in to the horizon of his lap.

Bobby's fingers get stuck in her sprayed blonde mop. He stares at the intentional dark roots and the scattered pink plastic barrettes. She twists the neck of his t-shirt in her fist as she bends down to bite her nails.

His stubble floats in the bath even though she has drawn a fresh one. She leaves their only mirror propped in the corner of the white tub. She steps into the bath, squealing. As her shoulders shiver, her shins turn fuschia. Slowly, she squats down, the bony tips of her buttocks and the lowest curl of her pubic hair scalding. She looks hard in the mirror, plastering her hair back to squeeze a couple of pimples on her forehead. There are smaller ones on her cheeks and chin, but she only squeezes the big ones. Two bits of blood make a vampire's kiss near her left temple. She quickly sits and lies back. A wave hits the faucets and splashes on to the mottled, frameless mirror. Beads of sweat form on her brow. She takes a couple of deep breaths then lifts her right leg in a *grande battement*, pointing her toes. Hairy, she thinks, scars. She lowers the leg onto the corner beside the faucet not occupied by the mirror. The corner leads out of the bath and her toes drip water onto the brown and orange floor tiles. She lifts her left leg and crosses it over her right ankle, digging her right heel's calluses into a muck of old green soap.

Zits, she thinks, scars, hair, little red bumps under the arms, stretch marks on the hips, corns on the feet, what next? Axe's chlamydia? a yeast infection? AIDS? She stares at the grey grunge framing the cracked blue bathroom tiles. Maybe it is catching. Decay. She never looked like this when she was rich. She had perfect skin then. Tanned. But she was fat until ballet lessons taught her the art of anorexia, a discipline that stripping has honed to a craft. Six of one, half a dozen of the other. But what if it was true that perfection was possible? She could go to a dermatologist, she could do masks and pedicures, and sleep more than five hours a night, and eat things like kelp and bee pollen. It was probably too late. The damage was done.

Nobody seemed to care but her anyway. And Bobby would laugh at her. Perfection is pointless, he said. But he thought everything was pointless. He was no authority. He would be a dishwasher the rest of his life. Not because he wanted the simple life but because he didn't want any other kind of life either. He was pointless, an unsharpened pencil, a broken needle going around and around the same warped record.

A dramatic crash interrupts her musing. She shrieks gleefully with surprise. The mirror has slipped into the bath and smashed underneath the water, spraying shards of glass. Bobby bursts through the door, breaking the latch. He is shaking, his last girlfriend had slit her wrists in the bath. He stands there looking at the large fragments of mirror under the bridge of her legs. "Shit, I knew this was going to happen eventually. I should have put it on the floor after I shaved."

She hadn't moved a centimetre, even during the first shock of it. She remains still. Some tiny pieces glitter on the surface of the water. She feels a pricking in her thigh. She reaches down and pulls a small blade of glass out. A little trickle of blood drips into the water where it buds and unfurls. Bobby leans over, putting one arm under her legs and one around her back. He groans as he picks her up and deposits her on the floor. She sits on the dirty green bathmat with her knees up against her chest. She laces her fingers in between her toes and leans against the bath. As he picks pieces of the mirror out of the water and stacks them on the edge of the tub, she is swimming on the surface of a fierce clear joy. Unreflective and pointless.

Fucking great, he thinks. No food, no money to get to work. He is going to have to leave an hour early to walk there. If he could learn to eat cockroaches, he'd have a feast to fuel him for the journey. Their one-bedroom is filled with empty packages — chip bags, cigarette packs, beer bottles, pizza cartons, 7-11 Big Gulp cups, styrofoam coffee cups. It makes him hungry.

She always does this. Just takes off and doesn't even leave a note. Where the hell is she? It is futile to even ponder the question. She could be anywhere, with anyone. Doing anything.

Well, he'd get paid tonight and take her out for dinner if she showed up after work. Maybe he'd have cause for celebration. Maybe he'd get promoted to prep cook. He wouldn't mind that. At least one of them would know how to boil rice without burning the shit out of it and having to throw the pot out into the alley.

He pictures himself at the prep counter with a big knife flashing out from his hand. No way could he do that. He'd cut his fucking thumb off. Selena would want to make the bones into a necklace.

No way he'd get the job anyway. They'd hire someone straight out of college. Or someone with experience cooking. He remembered trying to find this job. At telemarketing places he was told he wasn't dressed appropriately enough to talk on the phone. They wanted him to have grade twelve to be a liquor store clerk or a sanitation engineer. And landscaping businesses wanted him to have three years experience mowing lawns. As if he'd ever lived in a house with a lawn and a mower. He was lucky Axe had gotten him this restaurant job. They'd wanted experience too. As if washing dishes was a skill requiring years of practice and training. Pathetic. He puts his cracked old leather jacket on and starts doing up his Grebs. Then he has to find his keys. He finally sees them on the back of the toilet, beside a dead plant.

He'd wanted plants in their place. Live ones. It was the first time he'd lived with only one other person. A chance to stretch out. Unroll ideas about how he might want a place to look. But it was the same old thing. Furniture scavenged from garbages, a futon on the floor that attracted mice, Salvation Army pink blankets. Paint was expensive, but some plants might have made the apartment more colourful, more alive. She'd said, "Oh, houseplants are so Seventies nouveau riche back-to-nature. They remind me of brown shag carpeting and macramé plant holders in hideous shades of green."

He leaves a note: *Gone to work. Payday. Meet me there at 2:30? We can go to Fran's or someplace for dinner.* And leaves the building. He walks hunched over, his hands gloveless and curled in his pockets. His keys fall out of a hole in the fabric. He bends down and picks them out of the snow, putting them in his jeans. A sharp wind blows snow from the top of a big pile towards him. He crosses his arms in front of him to keep his buttonless coat closed.

She'd like big plants in ornate containers, he'd bet. Hotel lobby plants. That's probably what it was like at her family's house. She was so self-styled. Poverty as a pose. A performance even. Inscribing her individuality for the benefit of public audiences. It transfixed him. Held him captive in the iridescent wound of her need to be noticed. Freed him from ever having to believe what she said. Like that shit about her dad locking her up in a private nuthouse in California when her mother ran away to India. Like that shit about her escaping the nuthouse and easy-riding across the States with a gang of bikers. Like that shit about how, no matter what she did, she would love him forever and ever, cross her heart and hope to die.

"Yo, Bobby!" A huge potbelly butts him in the elbow. "Hey, I got the assistant cook job!"

Bobby turns to the Jamaican woman beaming down at him, "How the hell did you do that, Weeze?"

"I took a night course in Thai cooking." Louise holds her purple mittens over her ears so he has to yell into the wind as they walk up the alley.

"How did you do that?"

"I got a student loan. It paid for the course. You should do the same thing."

"Yeah, but you have to pay it back, with interest."

"You make more. You can pay it back in a couple of years."

"Well, I'm glad you got the job."

"Thanks."

They walk into the contrived slapdash style of the tropical restaurant. Bobby takes Louise's coat and bag. She runs into the kitchen then comes back out, "Hey, Bobby, while you're taking our shit upstairs, could you bring down a pail of squid?"

"Sure."

Bobby walks up the old fire escape and into the little room at the top. He throws the coats on some boxes and opens the door of the freezer. He starts carrying the heavy pail out, splashing ice on the floor. He takes a rest on the balcony. He looks down. The owner's little ponytail bobs up and down as he snorts some coke off his finger, then takes a baggie from a guy in a black turtleneck. Bobby lifts the pail up and holds it to his chest. Very slowly, he starts down the first step. Then the second. Some grey slime spills over the rim of the pail. The nerves in his forearm are buzzing. He can't look down over the swamp of butchered squid. He imagines trying to put them back together again and leading them hand-in-hand down the stairs. He makes two more steps safely, then stumbles. The bucket tips over the railing, showering the owner and his friend with squid and slime.

Bobby's muscles are twitching to run, but his eyes are mesmerized, replaying the moment of the fall superimposed on the vision of his boss wet and squirming with greyish purple squiggles. They all stand stunned for about three seconds. Then his boss yells, "*What. Is. Your. Name.*"

Bobby begins to laugh so hard he can't speak, "Aieeee, Aieee, Aiee, Ack, Ackse, Axe. My name is Axe. I know, I'm fired."

He goes back upstairs to get his coat. The owner is still yelling, "*Jesus. Fucking. Christ. Somebody. Clean. This. Up.*"

Selena shuffles up the circular driveway at Havergal College. She skips up the steps and sits beside a chubby girl with dark brown braids under a green beret. "Hey, Courtney."

"Dad is coming to pick me up. We'll get in trouble." Courtney tugs Selena's miniskirt down further along the thigh next to her.

"We have a couple of minutes. How are you?" Selena takes Courtney's beret and puts it on.

"We're going to Europe tomorrow."

"Yeah, I remember you telling me last week." Selena puts the beret back on Courtney's head.

Courtney squints. "You look different."

"Ugly. I'm not wearing make-up. I have to get a new mirror."

"No, just different."

"So, I guess you're excited about this trip, huh. I remember when Dad took me a couple of times. Mostly I had to stay in the hotel while he went to meetings. But he took me to the Louvre and the Eiffel Tower. I almost puked, it was so high."

"My mom is coming too. She said we could go anywhere we want."

"Well, that's better then. Hey," Selena reaches out her hands, "Can I borrow your house key when you're gone? You won't need it and you could say you lost it."

Courtney screws up her face, "What do you want it for?"

"Just wanted a look at the old place, you know, remember being a kid and everything. Don't worry, you won't get in shit. Dad will never know I was there."

"Do you know the alarm number?"

"5274, right?"

"Nooo. It's my birthday now so I won't forget it."

"Oh, that's easy, November the twenty-ninth, 1129."

"Yeah," Courtney gives her a key on a Las Vegas key chain.

"Where'd you get this?" Selena holds the key chain up and a showgirl kicks her leg.

"Oh, Dad goes there sometimes. It makes Mom mad."

"What are you doing in math now?"

"Adding and subtracting fractions."

"Want me to show you when you get back?"

"Okay." Courtney takes the key and zips it into the pocket of Selena's jacket, "Lots of zippers. There's the key. You better go now."

Selena makes no move to leave. She sits, feeling the fear tease her. The possibility of seeing him, after four years. Seeing his lips press into a straight line, his eyes picking and chipping at her, trying to mine her for the daughter that would please him. Each time she would try to hold out and fail. She would try to see herself growing bigger under his stare, big enough to expand beyond the limits of his vision. She jumps up.

A BMW had pulled into the driveway. A woman driver.

Courtney remains seated. "You never know what he's going to be driving. That could have been him. You better go now."

"Yeah, see ya." Selena doesn't even look at Courtney as she leaves. She can feel her heart beating hard at the base of her throat, a choking fist pounding. All of her nerves are twitching and buzzing. She is being electrocuted by her own nervous system, eaten alive by her own hive of synaptic hornets. Shit, she'd never be able to palm a mirror today.

Bobby kneels on the floor to take off his boots. "I got bad news."

"You got fired." Selena leans against the kitchen counter.

"Yeah, and I got good news."

"How you got fired."

"Shit! How did you know?"

"Axe called. He's fired too. He doesn't know why except maybe because he recommended you. He wants to write a song called *Squidding the Boss*."

"It's my story."

"Yeah, well you have to tell Axe that."

"Forget it, it's not important."

Selena walks over to the phone. She picks it up and dials.

"What are you doing? Selena. Don't. Please."

"Hi, Axe. Hey, forget about that song. Bobby's already written one.... No, I don't think we'll go to the speak tonight... I don't care... we don't have any money... I just don't feel like it...." She hangs up suddenly, turning to Bobby, "You don't want to go to Tanya's speak tonight do you?"

"We don't have any money."

"We could call up Jules and Layla. Or Purple Mike. They'd buy us drinks."

"I don't feel like it."

"Neither do I. But what else is there to do?"
"I'm kind of tired."
"I think I'll stay up and just smoke."
"Goodnight."
"Yeah."

Selena feels extremely conspicuous walking along the Bridle
Path. Nobody walks here, everybody drives everywhere. She
turns on to a tree-lined driveway and walks up to a huge
white colonial house. She goes around to the side door and
lets herself in, quickly pressing the alarm number after she
closes the door behind her. That smell. New car, dry-cleaned
suit, lemon oil and Hollandaise. She takes little steps in, brushing and wiping off snow. The gardener could be around the
corner, or a maid. Each foot forward could tip her over into
nothingness. Whatever lived behind the dream that was this
house. Her dream, because it had been her home. But mostly
some collective dream of how things should be.

She tiptoes in her high-heeled boots through the kitchen
and up a wrought-iron spiral staircase. She will not turn left
towards her old rooms, she will not. She turns right and walks
by the hall mirror. It is the first time she has seen herself full-
length for a long time. With her roots showing, her lack of
make-up, her tattered leopard-print coat, her scuffed and salt-
stained boots, she looks like a prostitute paid in video game
quarters, young enough to have skinned knees and mosquito
bites dotted with pink lotion.

After making a face, she moves on down the hall to the
yellow master bedroom. She goes into her father's dressing
room and opens an ornately carved wooden box on his bureau.
She counts the money, $2459. She takes a thousand and puts it
in her pocket. He might not even notice it's missing.

I've saved him a lot of money, she thinks, I've been supporting myself since I was sixteen. He owes me at least a thousand. This is my fucking trust fund.

She hurries back to the kitchen and sits in the wood phone
booth. Above the intercom is a row of brass hooks. About
twenty keys hang here. She finds the one labeled AH and takes
it. Then she goes out to the garage. Luckily, the Austin Healey
is one of the cars in front of the door. She presses the button
to unroll the door. She gets in the Austin Healey, assessing its
pedals and knobs. Shit. She's forgotten how to drive standard.

Selena comes bursting into the apartment as Bobby is hanging up the phone.

"Come on, get packed."

"What are you talking about? We have a gig this weekend.
Where could we go anyway?"

"For fuck's sake, just pack all your sweaters, okay? We have
to get out of town. Now."

"Why?"

"You'll see. Don't be such a drag."

She flies into the bedroom and starts stuffing clothes from
the floor into their laundry bag.

Bobby puts his coat and boots on. "Did something bad
happen?"

"No, something good happened. Come see."

Selena starts running out of the apartment and down the
narrow stairs. Bobby follows her. She opens the door of a
black sports car and shoves the laundry bag in the back seat.

"Did you steal this?"

"Yeah, come on."

She screams all the way around and up the ramp on to the 401 eastbound. Then she turns the radio up. Every five seconds he says, "There's a cop!"

"The thing is," she says, "sometimes you have to shake things up so that they'll settle into a new arrangement of circumstances."

"Like jail. Jail would be a new circumstance."

"I keep telling you, people steal cars all the time. We are not going to get caught. In three hours we'll be there. It's already dark. The chances of us getting caught on the way are toothpick slim."

"And toothpick pointy."

"Oh good, they're playing Sonic Youth." She turns the radio up.

They pull up at a gap in the line of trees beside the unplowed old road. Snow is falling thick and heavy in the beams of the headlights, which bounce off the windows of the house. She turns the ignition off. The car won't make it into the drive-way. The windows go black again and she stops trembling. They step out and sink above their knees in snow. Bobby shoulders the laundry bag as Selena leads the way. Each step a chore. It takes about twenty minutes to reach the sprawling Victorian house. In the Queen Anne style, the house favors its north corner, towards the bay, with a three-tiered turret topped with a domed balcony. The south corner angles out like a back-facing triptych. Bobby can't set the bag down on the front porch because even there the snow is deep. He hunches around his burden in the moonlight that escapes the talons of the fancy wood tracery hemming the roof of the porch. Selena takes an old key out of her pocket and opens the front door.

She holds her lighter up to find the light switch. She doesn't know if the utilities are still connected. They are. Bobby puts the laundry bag down and bends to take off his boots. His fingertips are numb. When he stands again, she is gone.

He walks into the living room, shivering. He turns on a Tiffany lamp that is discernible in front of the window. Dust falls on the sleeve of his coat. He starts pulling white sheets off the furniture. The room looks as if it hadn't been touched since some age worthy of nostalgia. It makes him think of people in flowing white tennis clothes arranging flowers and having tea, the legacy of Agatha Christie movies on TV. It is packed with curios and knickknacks that seem as if they hadn't been bought but had grown out of the expected generosity of the house itself. Selena comes in.

"It's weird. I turned on the furnace and the water. Why would the power still be on? It'll take the whole night to warm this place up. We better get a fire going. You open the flue and I'll go get wood from the shed."

He goes over to the fireplace. He'd only seen them on television. He can't figure out how to open the flue. He doesn't even know what a flue is.

She comes back and starts a fire. The room fills with woodsmoke. She reaches in and pulls the lever to open the flue.

"Let's go into the kitchen."

The kitchen is enormous, with an old wood stove and a gas stove from the Thirties that is as big as two new stoves. He sits at the big wood table as she makes tea. "I found cans of corn, beans, condensed milk, beets, soup. But we'll have to go into town tomorrow for eggs, milk, bread, juice...."

He remains silent. He does not know how to be. He has never seen her be efficient. He has never been in a place like this. He has never even been outside of Toronto.

They take their tea and condensed milk into the living room and sit on the floor in front of the fireplace. Selena gets a saucer to use as an ashtray and they light cigarettes. It is warm enough to take off their coats. Bobby unlaces her boots and peels them off.

The fire reminds her of a rainy fall day when she was little. She'd been outside in her wellies and a tie-dyed t-shirt and no underpants, collecting worms and shivering and waiting to be let back in the house. Her mother had finally called her in, her long blonde hair swinging against the open door and brushing the top of Selena's brown bowl cut as Selena shimmied under her outstretched arm and into the house.

"Ta-da!" her mother had said, escorting her into the living room. A fire was roaring and in front of it were placed two beach towels under a red and white striped umbrella. A portable radio played Fleetwood Mac. "We're having a lovely sunny day at the beach."

She took the handful of worms from Selena's fat cupped palm and threw them on the fire, where they shriveled out a dank and bitter little scent that curled up into the sweet haze of pot smoke and woodsmoke.

Selena lay on one of the beach towels as her mother took off her boots and t-shirt and rubbed her all coconutty and buttery with suntan lotion. They lay there naked and giggling, sometimes getting up to dance to a song for an appreciative, if invisible, audience, until finally falling asleep late into the night.

Selena caught pneumonia.

She shivers a bit and turns to Bobby, wanting to make him know, if not this particular thing, then something. She says, "This was my grandmother's house. My mother inherited it. I don't know where she is really. But my stepmother said she was in some mental institution in California. And Dad told me I was as crazy as my mother when he kicked me out for running away from boarding school. So maybe it's true. But it could all be lies."

This is the most history he has ever heard her speak to him alone. And without the role, the fanfare, the audience to play for, all the things that usually required her insincerity. As she falls silent, he doubts he will get to hear more. She refuses to look at him and he assumes her embarrassment. Suddenly she asks, "What's your last name?"

"It was Flynn until I was adopted by the Dowdalls when I was twelve."

"The Dowdalls were the born-agains, right?"

"Yeah."

She looks at him then, the firelight carving cheekbones into her round cheeks. Her eyes seemed rabbitty at first, without their make-up. Lashless and pink-rimmed. But now they seem to define themselves by their large size alone. Unblinking, and in all seriousness, she proffers a dirty-nailed hand and says, "Hi, I'm Selena Rose Bradshaw-Smith."

He shakes her hand awkwardly. "Hi, I'm Bobby Flynn."

She keeps his hand and places it at the base of her throat. He can feel her pulse, rabbits leaping through a boa constrictor. She takes his hand again and holds it as she lays down and uses her other hand to pull the white sheets around her. She lays her head down on her coat and falls asleep sucking on his index finger. He stays up the whole night, seldom taking his eyes from the fire fading from her hair.

As she trudges down the drive to the car, she hears barking. She turns around slowly but can't see a dog. She goes on, trying to use her bootsteps from the previous night. She squints into the glare of sun reflecting off the snow. She can sense a disturbance in the scruffy cedars to her right. A black shadow rolls to her feet. She looks down. A dog writhes epileptically down deeper into the snow. She bends and pats his head, scratching behind his ear. His fur is coarse and prickly. She continues patting and scratching down his back. He stands to shake the snow off but falls over. She puts her arm around him and rights him. She smoothes her hand down his left side to wipe off the snow. When she gets to his back left leg, she finds a stump. It makes her fingers shiver and recoil.

"I have to go into town. I'll be back soon."

He tries to follow her with his strange jerky walk, but the snow is too much of a challenge.

She will buy some dog food in town.

The dog spins backwards in circles until he knocks over a kitchen chair. Bobby rights it and slumps down to the floor to gentle the dog into his lap. He won't look at Selena, who is pouring kibble into a silver bowl. The dog can't take his eyes off her.

Bobby shoots a look at her finally, his face definite and rare. "No, you can't feed him."

"What do you mean? Why not?" Selena, always shocked when he refuses her, is doubly shocked that he is attempting to refuse her this. "Look how skinny he is."

"If you feed him, he'll stick around."

"So?"

"So, you can't afford to feed a dog for long. And are you really going to walk him every day and give him baths and take him to the vet for shots and get him fixed? Can you really take care of a pet?"

"Well I don't know until I try."

"He's not an experiment, he's a living thing. Just wait, he'll go back where he came from."

"I asked in town. They've seen him around but no-one owns him. He'll starve."

"No. Forget it. It's not fair. I'm not letting you make a big fuss over this dog and then fuck him up. We'll take him into town when we leave if he's still hanging around. Someone will take him in. Someone who can take care of him."

"Come on, let's go."

"Home?"

"No, I'm taking you someplace. I hope they're still there."

Selena puts on the old fur coat she found in the hall closet. Bobby's boots had started to leak so she'd bought them both Wellingtons and thick work socks. They put them on and go out to the car.

"Here, Twitch, come on boy."

The dog scatters snow across the small back seat before settling down. Bobby twists around the passenger seat to pat him as Selena warms the engine up. The dog looks like him — wiry, bigger than he seems, prickly tufts of dark hair, round brown eyes edged with tarnished gold. Twitch shakes the whole way. Selena keeps the windshield wipers going and drives slowly the whole way. It is still snowing and the plow hasn't come through since the second night.

"Look, Selena," Bobby points to a giant Santa, complete with sleigh and a string of reindeer, erected on the roof of one of those houses that were once trailers.

"Maybe they leave it up all year. It must be hard to put up."

"The Dowdalls thought that Santa was sacrilegious. Old Nick, Saint Nick, what's the difference."

"Didn't you get presents anyway?"

"Not really. Stuff I needed. Socks, long underwear, plaid shirts, a polyester brown suit to wear to church. Maybe that's why I wanted to invent toys. I used to draw plans for flying boats and things."

"I wanted to be a gardener. I used to follow our gardener around and get all dirty helping him weed and plant. I used to make him order special flowers from the catalogue for my own bed. Aster Prinette, California Poppy Mission Bells, Songbird Robin. My favourite was the Magpie Aquilegia. It had this cup of black petals with white edges and then a sort of spiky frame of really dark maroon petals. Like wine."

Selena turns left on to a bridge that arches up to the sky. It looks like the car will fly right off it. They look to the right and see ice-fishing huts speckling the lake like flies on a bed-sheet. Then they head downwards.

She pulls into the parking lot of the Native Renaissance store and tells Twitch he'll have to wait in the car a while.

"Do you want to go in? They have jewelry and clothes and touristy stuff mostly. But they also have some carvings and paintings."

"I wouldn't mind taking a look."

"Well, I'll be out back where the cougars are."

Selena squats a long time in front of the cage, but she can't see any cougars. She is about to give up when she becomes aware of a cougar face peering over a short wall of cement bricks in a dark corner of the cage. The blue eyes stare at her — cold, feral, fierce. She feels a fear that is mostly awe. The cougar comes around the wall and starts walking slowly towards her. She is sure it is going to leap at the fence in front of her. She braces herself. The cougar pauses and scrunches up her face. Her pupils dilate and she looks at Selena as if in love with her. The cougar begins to rub her face against the fence, as if it is Selena's hand. Selena looks back intently, fully. She hears Bobby's shuffle through the snow and the cooing of pigeons on the roof of the store behind her. The cougar's mate emerges alongside her. He too stares at Selena as Bobby squats beside her. The female cougar stops rubbing her face against the fence. She licks her lips with a plump, not pointed, tongue. Her mate puts his arm around her shoulders, bends his head down, and kisses her neck.

Selena is unaware that her eyes are wet. She is only conscious of the cougars. She watches the yellow stream of urine spray from the male's penis. She watches the female wash her front paws and then leap on to a plywood platform. Bobby watches Selena. And then, when she stands up and starts walking back towards the car, he follows her.

The moisture under her eyes starts to freeze, stinging her dark circles. I've been crying, she thinks, weird. Maybe it's the cage. Or maybe it's that once she'd seen her father kiss her mother like that, with the same sensation of watching them as if from behind a chain-link fence. Or maybe it's just because the cougars were still there. She doesn't know why. It is probably just random sadness. The weather. PMS.

"We have to go home tonight. I have to get the car back to my Dad's before he returns from Europe."

They ride back without speaking. Selena watches the road and wonders why she told him. It had slipped out so easily. It had suspended her belief in her own fictions. There is something about him that makes such fictions seem unnecessary, even vaguely embarrassing.

Bobby listens to Twitch's tail hitting the leather upholstery and the wind blowing snow into the window. He thinks about what she has said. She hadn't stolen the car, not really. He had negotiated the terror of getting caught for no reason. This doesn't make him angry. It only serves to make him admire even more her art of embellishment. And it makes him happy to finally be part of its inner workings.

They towel off Twitch in the hall and then round up their belongings. Bobby thinks he sees Selena slip some small objects wrapped in linen napkins into the laundry bag. She goes into the kitchen and he follows. She begins doing the dishes. He sits at the table, stroking Twitch's head on his lap, and watches her. The pale green dishes are scalloped around the edges and the rims are decorated with lacy patterns of gold, like old birdcage metalwork. She washes them one at a time in the water instead of piling them in. She even washes the backs of the plates and the bottoms of the teacups. He has never seen her take such care with anything. He thinks about offering to dry, but he doesn't want to interrupt her ritual.

When she scrapes a pot of purple cabbage stew into the garbage, he thinks about how he's lost his job. He doesn't want to go on Welfare. He starts tapping his foot. Twitch gets up and wanders into the living room. He decides to follow. He begins throwing the sheets back on the furniture, which is dusty anyway. On a couple of endtables and on the mantelpiece are spots that are free of dust among the china eggs, the silver jars of rose petals, the porcelain bowls of seashells, the vases of rose glass. Every object assumes the guise of something else. A lamp is a Greek goddess. Bookends are brass sailing ships. He keeps thinking about the pail of squid.

Selena finishes putting all the dishes in the glass-doored cabinet. She ties the garbage bag and goes to place it with the laundry bag so she will remember to take it with her and stop at the dump on the way back. She peeks into the living room. Bobby is squatting on a sheet spread across the large oriental carpet. He is leaning forward and writing on the sheet with the black marker he keeps on his person for graffiti purposes.

"What are you doing?"

"Finishing that song. There."

"Can I see it?"

"When we get back."

He starts balling up the sheet.

"What are we going to do with the gramophone? It doesn't have a cover now."

"We'll play it." Bobby goes over and turns the crank. Then he wipes a record from one of the shelves in the gramophone's cabinet and opens the door to the speaker. He puts the record down on the spinning disk, the weight of the 78 slowing the disk a little. Then he puts the needle arm down.

The song is called 'Havana is Calling Me', a Cuban rumba. He goes over to Selena and takes her hands. They spin awkwardly around the room as the record slows, and then Selena goes over and pumps the crank around furiously. The voice becomes squeaky and the Spanish phrasing indecipherable. Selena pretends to gather up a long skirt and swish it around, her hips hyperactive. But when the record slows again she lets Bobby just stand and hold her, the tip of her nose clinking the rings in his ear together.

A KICK

It was more than just a bad day. I woke up and she'd left, leaving this drawing on the pillow. She'd magic markered it right on the pillow, this drawing, and it was of a girl, I mean woman, lying on her side crying her eyeballs out in smeary black magic marker, and behind this girl, but really looking like he's floating over her, is this naked guy lying on his side with his arm elbowed up and his head resting on that hand, and he's smoking a cigarette and staring into space all blasé and whatever. So I guess I was really drunk last night.

And the thing that really got me was that the guy was wearing this old hat like the one I wear with the rip in the brim, a fedora, that she says makes me look like a bum, like that's something to be avoided, like that's wrong for some reason, not done, and something about the guy smoking in this hat and staring away reminded me of my dad and it made me kind of sick. I mean it's no big deal, I haven't seen him in years and I'm completely indifferent about the guy. I never think about him or anything. And I felt kind of sick. It was probably the hangover.

So now I had to sleep on this raw pillow, without that thing that covers the pillow, because this drawing makes me sick. I had to take the thing off she'd drawn on, and I know I'm just never going to bother going to Goodwill for another one. I tried to go back to sleep with the raw pillow, you could still see the drawing sort of, because the marker went right through the thing onto the pillow, but splotchy and blurry enough so you couldn't really tell what it was, but it was all slippery and so I couldn't go back to sleep. And some of the ink must have been wet still because I got all of these black smudges on my face that wouldn't come off.

I tried to clean myself up because I had a job interview, and I shaved and everything but still looked ratty, so I decided not to worry about it. There was nothing I could do about it so, fuck. So I got to the restaurant early for this job and there were maybe twenty-five people already there, and it turns out that the job's three shifts a week, at minimum wage, so even if I beat everyone out and got the job I still couldn't support myself. The guy was this real patronizing slick-ass too, and he laughed at my school certificate and resumé of ten years' experience — I've been working since I quit high school at fifteen and I worked my way through cooking school too — and he said he might have a part-time dishwashing shift coming up in a few weeks. Dishwashing. And I found out later from this friend who'd worked there that this guy never went to school or worked, his dad bought him the restaurant as soon as he graduated grade twelve and he hardly ever did anything useful there, being basically paid to cause problems for someone other than his dad.

Then I got home and Jim said he was moving in with his girlfriend, and since his name was the one on the lease and all the utilities this meant that we'd have to convince the landlord to give one of us a new lease, and the landlord hated us, so this didn't look good, and the vacancy rate is 0.01%, so this wasn't good. Jim said he wanted his name off of everything regardless, and by the way there's a letter for you on the kitchen counter.

I found the letter under a pot of water with bubbles of mould clinging to the sides. I didn't know water could go bad. It was from my bank. It said that they'd been trying to reach me by phone for weeks but I wasn't returning their calls — nobody gives me my messages — and I had to pay back my whole entire student loan right this fucking minute or I was fucking dead. I phoned them because I'm supposed to have a six month grace period, but they said I'd had it already so the school must have put the wrong date on those forms. I phoned the school but no-one knew anything or knew anyone who knew anything and they told me to phone the bank. I phoned the bank again and they told me to phone the student loan people at the government, then I spent two hours getting through to them and they told me to talk to the school, which was now closed. I was in a really bad mood.

Then my mom showed up and paid me back the fifty bucks I'd lent her, and she felt really bad about taking so long but I couldn't deal with making her feel better right then, so I said I had to meet somebody and put her on the subway.

I went to the bar and ran into Jim and Jane and Petra and Kisa and that whole gang from The Chlamydia Club, but I wouldn't sit with them because I wanted to be alone and have just one beer and go home and read, so now they all probably hate me. And I ended up having maybe thirteen beers somehow and blew it in the end by getting into this big argument with this guy about economics, which I know nothing about, but this guy was a total fucking bastard who assumes that because he has a BA he'd be hanging with the rich people as the rest of us all got poorer. Yeah, right. None of my friends with BAs can get jobs, which is why I did cooking at George Brown instead of film school, because there were still supposed to be jobs in the trades.

So I got really pissed and was walking home still arguing with this guy in my head, except even in my head he still wasn't really listening to me, when I passed my bank. I stopped for a minute, staring in at the arrangement of red velvet ropes and the backs of all the clean computer terminals, and I noticed a blinking red light over a video camera pointed directly at me. This looked like opportunity. With all the show I could muster, I stuck my middle finger straight up in its smug Big Brother face. But somehow this just made me feel stupid and useless. The camera kept staring at me all impassive, and like I give a fuck, and so what.

So I kicked the glass wall between us with all kinds of force I'd never suspected and ended up on my ass, half in and half out of the bank, with glass wailing all around me and a big siren smashing out of the place. I tried to get up and run but my leg wouldn't go and was all bloody, and then a cop was standing over me all mad.

I was arrested for all kinds of things and sewn up and bandaged and plea-bargained down to vandalism. I had to borrow money to pay for the window, and they wouldn't give me disability welfare, and I was on crutches for a few weeks. Tanya broke up with me because I didn't call her to come take care of me when my leg was really bad. Anyway the whole thing was fucking stupid and shows what a big asshole loser I am. I'll probably never live it down.

But I get kind of happy when I remember my boot going through the window. First my boot's on the sidewalk, then up in the air, then it meets the window, then the window breaks, then the boot is inside. I meant to smash the window and I kicked it and the window broke. A predictable cause and effect relationship. Not like I go back to school to get a job, I go to school and work my ass off and don't get a job. With that window, what I tried to do worked.

And there was this one great flash when the window broke and the alarm went off, as I was falling back to the ground, this one great flash of straight clean triumph. For that one second, I felt like I'd really made a point.

It was an old early Seventies bottle of 7Up that started it. There the bottle was, lying in the gutter, oblivious to the tires swerving dangerously close. He was about to sweep it into his bag when the first ray of spring glinted off it as green as a puddle of moss back home in Muskoka. He bent down and picked it up, this gift from the gutter of Toronto. The red and white lettering on the green glass reminded him of Christmas. He noticed a line of plain white capital letters ringing the bottom. He sat down and squinted at it, resting his broom on his shoulder. It said: YOU LIKE IT, IT LIKES YOU! He repeated this out loud three times, dusting off the glass. He put the bottle in his pocket and took it back to the rooming house after work.

He sat down on the edge of the sagging bed and looked at it perched on the old brown dresser. It was the only colour in the room. The walls were tan, the bed was an old rusty iron hospital bed, and his only personal possession was a dusty grey footlocker under the window. Even the view was monotonous. All that could be seen through the grimy panes was a wall of crumbling, bloody mud brick. The room fit him like fingerless gloves on a man whose hands were too large for available sizes. Luke himself had sepia skin and tobacco hair and old leather button eyes. But this wasn't the only thing that made the fit so neat. It was the small dimensions of the room and the way the coughing, spitting, scratching, heaving noises of the other residents were at once so intimate and so removed.

Luke did not have a life. He had a fog of muted colours and muffled sounds, and this fog stood between him and the life that belonged to him. He didn't describe this to anyone, or how he could see the lives of others, brightly animate with clear outlines, just beyond his reach. He described it to himself often. It was like chain-smoking in front of a television in a dark room. The purpose of repeating this description, or analogy, was to remind himself not to take this state for granted, and thus not to accept it as uncritically assumed reality.

However, this bottle, with its red and green and white and its enigmatic message, somehow had entered his room without losing its colour. He didn't know how to fit it into his description. He couldn't figure the slogan out at all. Was the 7Up saying that you like it, therefore it will like you back, a proposal of conditional affection that was as if the bottle was either desperate for approval or simply undiscriminating in its tastes? Or was it that you like it because it likes you, playing on your own self-interested motive for appreciation? But how could pop and/or (what does 'It' actually refer to?) its container demonstrate its affection for you? By tasting good? Edibility as evidence of approval? If it didn't like you, would it taste bad? How did this message fulfill the requirements of the psychology of selling, the demands of seduction and desire? If you thoughtlessly accepted the words without attempting a logical connection between them — 'it', 'you', 'like' — would you then somehow feel a vague but positive relationship with the product and so purchase it? In the end, attempting to formulate a logical construction was disrupted by the mysteriousness of a comma, rather than a conjunction, connecting the two thoughts. This comma was determined to render the seemingly bald statement a riddle, a kind of zen koan. He decided to take the bottle to the Beverly Tavern and show it to his friend Deirdre.

Deirdre was wiping his table when he came in. She had frizzy brown hair in a bushy ponytail and wore African jewelry with an embroidered Guatemalan peasant blouse and a sarong skirt from Thailand. She looked more like a world traveler than a waitress. Technically, she was not a waitress but an archivist. Her grant had run out in the middle of a folklore project. The bar helped her to collect more urban myths for her mentoring professor's collection as well as pay the rent. She sat down beside Luke. "Got any ID, kid?"

"No, but I remember my social insurance number."

"Good enough. When is your birthday, anyway? The next one must be nineteen. Or have you already had it?"

"I never tell anyone my birthday." No-one had wanted to know before. That was why he liked Deirdre.

"Come on, just tell me. I won't tell anybody."

He kept looking down at the dirty rag in her hand on the table. He was smiling, "No."

"Well, what's your astrology sign then?"

"I don't know."

"If you tell me your birthdate, I can tell you your sign," she wheedled, teasing, "I could refuse to serve you, you know. Why don't you just tell me?"

"Why don't you just forget about it? You only want to know because I won't tell you," he said, thinking about how he played with his dog when he was little and how the minute he let go of the frisbee his dog would take off with it and not return for hours.

"Yeah, and then I'll forget about it, so you might as well tell me."

"No, you don't forget anything." This was true, her memory was her art. He couldn't believe it when she had called out his name when he had first come in here six months ago. They had stood in line together at graduation three years ago and he had talked to her out of his nervousness. It was the first almost personal conversation he'd had there. The other students tended to ignore him with either resentment or disinterest because of his youth. They were never very real to him anyway, slouching technicolour characters flitting about the pages of books, afflicted with a tic-inflected echolalia, a halting and hesitant chorus whose hygiene deteriorated and revived with the semester cycle. But Deirdre had not ignored him. She had asked if he was the youngest person to graduate from the University of Toronto and he had said that he was one of them. That was it, besides the exchange of names and majors. She had gone on to do Museum Studies and he'd done a Masters in Philosophy and then gone back to his summer street-sweeping job for good. He didn't see the point in a Ph.D.

He had gone into philosophy because he thought this discipline might have something to say about the Meaning of Life, which was the only enduring topic he could consider worthy of pursuit. In any case, it was the only issue he found to be personally relevant. This approach had served him well as an undergraduate. He held 3 A.M. coffee klatches in his room with Kant and Hegel and Nietzsche and Heidegger. He was close to proving to himself that he existed when he entered his graduate program. It was at this point that his studies reached a crescendo in which all of the cumulative theoretical conflicts seemed to clash to the point of canceling each other out; the voices of the exalted dead in his head became frenzied and intoxicated, slurring incoherent snippets of non-sequiturs and bursting into dry operatic tears, and he began to forget what it was he was attempting to decipher the meaning of.

It was in a seminar with a prof infamous for chewing his wrist during his lectures to the point of drawing blood that the ignominy of Luke's own fall from ivory grace became apparent. The prof wrote the day's discussion question on the board and then stared pointedly at Luke while clamping down on his own humerus bone and commencing to gnaw. The question was: "Is life an economy box of kleenex perched on the back of a toilet, or is it a secondhand sparkplug sold as new by a conning auto mechanic of either gender?"

Luke blinked, a mark of possession by the spirit in the

rituals of some cultures, and replied offhandedly and abstract-edly, "Life is e-f-i-l spelled backwards."

In the humming silence he imagined applauded his answer, he saw it all stripped bare of any meaning — the words he used and those he didn't, the things, both abstract and concrete, that the words purported to refer to — all hollow, masking the sucking black hole hidden behind everything, a voracious and callous vacuum. Luke looked out the window. The sun shimmering up the spine of an autumn-proud tree was a sly and evil joke. He reeled with a clenching cold nausea that he couldn't laugh at any more. It was then that his prodigy intelligence forced him to accept the only surviving truism: that you could construct all the meanings you wanted but life itself was essentially meaningless. He settled into this premise with a complacency that was the first condition of simplicity he had ever known. There were to be no more pranks on his part. Only exercises. Empty, gestural, but sincere.

"Okay, fine, don't tell me. But I'll find out." Deirdre slanted her eyes. "I have my ways, you know."

She walked to the bar and brought back a Molson Canadian. He drank it from the bottle. He pulled out the 7Up bottle and handed it to her, "Look what I got."

She turned it over carefully, scrutinizing it as if preparing to catalogue it. She even looked into its small mouth with her right eye, as if the bottle were a telescope. She ran her fingers over the letters, reading out loud, "YOU LIKE IT, IT LIKES YOU! That's great. A real find. Did you get it on the street?"

"Yeah."

"You know, I think I remember these from when I was little. Yeah, yeah, I know. You could get these small bottles from an old Coca-Cola cooler that had a built-in opener. My dad has one of those coolers in his junkshop. But I didn't like 7Up, I liked Sprite."

"Do you like this bottle?"

"Yeah, I love it."

"You can have it." He tapped his foot nervously under the table.

"No, no, you keep it. I'm not just being polite, I mean it. It's a really cool bottle and I have so much junk it would get lost in it all."

After her refusal, a group of amateur hockey players came in and she had to get back to work. He felt funny. It was the first time he'd tried to give something to someone, and the fact that she hadn't accepted it made the attempt seem something of a failure. The bottle began to seem like an artifact of defeat. He finished his beer and left with the 7Up bottle dangling between two of his fingers the way cool guys in movies wielded beer bottles at pool parties. Deirdre waved as he was framed in the doorway, and in response he flipped the bottle up in the air and caught it behind his back. He was the secret master of many such gestures, but this public display that came so spontaneously embarrassed him in its testament to his lonely leisure hours and he slunk out immediately after.

On the way home he was tempted to smash it. But then he would have to sweep up the shards tomorrow when regret might appear. He could throw it in a garbage can and not have any evidence to remind him. He stood in front of a sticky-lipped container. He held the neck of the bottle sticking out of his army jacket pocket like a gunslinger with his hand on his holster. He could hear the smash of the 7Up bottle as it hit a pile of wine bottles deep in the nauseous bowels of the can. He could see the sanitation engineer pulling the black belly out the next morning and the daggers of glass inside slicing it open to spill all of its foul contents onto the sidewalk. He couldn't do it.

The whole five blocks home he kept his hand on the bottle

and worried that it would fall out of his pocket. He put it on the dresser again, in the very centre. He got into bed. It was like a crumpled paper bag whose crisp paper had softened from excessive use. He got up. He took the bottle back to bed with him, cradling it under his chin like a doorway sleeper.

The next day Luke picked up an old can of Tahiti Treat on Queen Street and a can of Jolt cola on University Avenue. He told himself that it was because he liked the palm trees and lightning bolt. He placed them on either side of the 7Up bottle on the dresser. He had woken up to find the bottle on the gritty floor and had panicked. It might have broken. He promised himself he wouldn't sleep with it any more. That night he woke up several times to check the silhouettes of the bottle and two cans on the dresser. The assemblage resembled a madman's crown.

After that, Luke brought home at least three cans every day. He never picked up a bottle again. He tried to when he found an old brown stubby beer bottle but he had a vague feeling of disloyalty and put it down. After work he would go to the Bev and show Deirdre his treasures. She told him that collectors never opened cans from the top because the tab was integral to the can. After that he bought his cans and learned to puncture the bottom, letting the liquid pour into a glass from the small opening.

Soon all of the regulars at the Bev were bringing him cans and calling him Popcan Man. He had a Pshitt pop from Yugoslavia and a Lucozade from Ireland and a Pokka Coffee from Japan. He had all of the major beverage corporations fully represented. For Coke alone he had five different sizes, an old can of denser metal, a New Taste Coke, a Coke Classic, a Caffeine Free, a Diet, a Sugar Free, a Caffeine and Sugar Free, a Cherry, a Lemon, a Japanese lettered, a Hebrew lettered, a British, a Christmas decorated, pull tabs and flip tabs. And he had Coke subsidiaries: Tab, Fresca, Mr. Pibb, Sprite, Diet Sprite. In addition to the popular brands he had rare specimens like Big Red, which was produced by Dr. Pepper; Champs Cola, which had a photo of Champion George Prince flexing his biceps; and Pete Chocolate Flavoured Beverage, which had a drawing of Pete Rose sliding into home. All four walls of his room were completely lined with red and green and yellow and blue cans. He was running out of room.

Luke was discussing this problem with Deirdre on one of her breaks. He had just purchased a Schwepps Cranberry Gingerale and a Pepsi Clear. She brought him glasses and tasted the liquids he drained from the cans.

"Yuck, they're both too sweet."

Luke never drank the contents of his cans. The act of draining them made the pop seem like a waste product, something to be eliminated and disposed of. He said, "If I got a different job I could move to a bigger place. But what kind of job can I get with a Masters in Philosophy? I'm not good at anything."

"I might have a simpler solution. You can worry about the job thing later. Why don't you let me archive your collection? You'll have photographs and descriptions of all your cans in your room so you can look at them any time you want and you can store the actual cans in my warehouse space. I could put it on my curriculum vitae somehow and it'll give me something to do while I wait for another project."

"I don't think so." Luke's hand clutched his new acquisitions. "I like having them around."

"Well, just let me archive them while you're looking for a new place just in case. C'mon, you'd be doing me a favor."

Luke thought about how he could carry his albums around with him and look at them on his breaks.

"Okay, come by this weekend. Here's the address. I'll meet you out front. But you can't have the cans. I'm still looking for a bigger place."

Luke led Deirdre up the dark stairs and into his cell. She had to sit on the bed because the collection made her dizzy and there was nowhere else to sit.

"What a dump. No wonder you want to keep your cans. But don't they overwhelm you? How can you live like this?"

Luke just stared at the 7Up bottle on the dresser and said, "YOU LIKE IT, IT LIKES YOU!"

"Well, it's too dim and crowded to shoot them in here. We'll have to take parts of the collection out and shoot them on the front steps before the house shadows them. Too bad the front yard is so full of weeds."

"You mean we have to take them all outside? I don't know about this." Luke turned the doorknob back and forth behind his back, "I mean, someone could steal some while we're making trips up and down the stairs and some could fall and get dented and I'd get the order all mixed up. No, I don't like this idea so much. Let's just forget the whole thing."

"Luke, don't be so neurotic. I know what I'm doing. I'm a professional. We'll just do the fruit juices today and tomorrow we'll start on the pops. It should take four weekends. Now, how do you want it catalogued? By companies or by types of drinks?"

"Both."

"Okay, I'll get doubles of all the pictures and do it both ways."

Luke hesitantly opened the door and let her out with her arms full of fruit juice cans.

The whole thing made him tired. Climbing up and down the stairs all day and then reconstructing the patterns. It was worrisome. But he had to admit she'd done a good job. He had five albums full. He decided to let her borrow the other five, the ones done by companies. Now he spent his weekends looking for a bachelor apartment. There were few he could afford. He put the album he'd been perusing back in his knapsack with the others and pulled the wire for the next stop. He put his sunglasses on as he got off the bus. The sun was blinding. If Deirdre had wanted to do the cataloguing now, in midsummer, he'd have definitely said no. The cans would have faded outside. He shuffled through bright green maple keys down towards the whisper of the waving lake. He checked the numbers of the houses and stopped at the last house before the park and the shore. He walked up its steep steps and rang the doorbell.

A suited man opened the door with a loud smile. He looked like the men in television ads for products with names like Suave and Preferred Stock. "Good morning! I'm glad you could make it! I'm Dan Travers. You must be... Luke Faring." He stuck out his hand to Luke without even blinking at Luke's torn jeans and stained white undershirt.

Luke shook his fingertips, surprised that they were real, and shoved his hands back in his pocket, wishing he could get the hang of these rituals. He tried and failed to say something.

Dan Travers pointed at his knapsack. "Ready to move right in, eh? Well, let's go take a look at the place. Right down these stairs. You said you were looking at a modest rent, right? Well, this is the place for you. I'll be frank with you, there's not much light, but with a beachfront property like this you can get all the sun you want just steps away! This is all-new broadloom in a neutral shade to go with any decor, just installed last week. It's a bit on the small side, but not for a bachelor apartment, and it's a self-contained unit with a private washroom."

Luke had trouble concentrating on the space. He watched Dan Travers make sweeping gestures and open little doors. It was like being little and thinking you could climb into the TV screen and be in there with the actors. Here he was in the screen with Dan Travers, who couldn't belong anywhere else that Luke knew of, and Luke suspected that Travers could put his hand right through Luke and Luke would disperse in a fog of white noise.

Luke forced himself to look around at the beige carpet and cream walls. Grey pipes webbed the ceiling neatly. He stayed hunched over. It was hardly bigger than his room and there was even less light, the only window the size of an open album and looking into a kind of pit dug into the backyard and lined with corrugated steel. Dan Travers was continuing his voice-over monologue, pointing at the bar-size fridge and the fake-wood cupboards above it. It smelled damp and musty. Luke felt a drop of liquid hit the part in his hair with a cold prick.

That was it. His cans would rust here.

"Well, it's very nice but, um, no."

"But wait, let me just show you the one bedroom for rent on the top floor. I know it's a little out of your price range but it's a real find, really unique. It would be perfect for someone like you."

Luke pondered this last statement as he followed Travers up stairs and more stairs. Until he suddenly believed that what was upstairs would illuminate and define him.

The sloping ceilings gave the tiny attic apartment, painted a vampish red, the impression of condensed intensity, as if it was pressurized and would explode if a match was lit or a window cracked open. Luke concluded that Dan Travers was full of shit. He was just a guy practicing his corporate graces on all and sundry at a dumb entry-level real estate job. He possessed no divine acuity that would match Luke with some kind of definition, or destiny, or even a home. He probably said "It would be perfect for someone like you" a dozen times a day.

Tuning out Dan Travers' never-ending sales pitch, Luke crawled into a tight corridor leading to a window and stared at the low angled ceiling above him. Some punk must have slept here for a while because there were anarchy symbols and political curses in magic marker faintly visible under the thin layer of fire alarm paint. He did kind of like this spot.

He thought of what it would be like to be the kind of person who lived in a red attic apartment. Someone passionate and direct, addicted to small dramas. Someone who at least lived as if his life mattered, whether it actually mattered or not being a moot point, a project to lively up their retirement years.

Luke thought of all his cans, how bright and shiny they were, how bold in their desire for attention, how simple in their geometric designs. They were a cornucopia of choices, suggesting infinite variations and combinations to satisfy any individual taste, hinting at endless possibilities. There would always be something new and improved. A new size, a new flavor, a new package. The promise of progress in each new improvement. However small, within the context of the collection these changes were significant variations on a theme. Eternal choice.

He thought of the bottle that began it all and sang its mantra under his breath. He wanted to be with his cans. He crawled back out of the alcove to see Dan Travers flipping his tie up and down nervously. Dan Travers cleared his throat and asked awkwardly, "Are you okay?"

This version of the man, somehow more tangible, as if Luke could smell the morning's sex and scrambled eggs under the deodorant and toothpaste, was even more discomfiting. Luke merely blinked his eyes, only once but elaborately, some signal intended to puzzle potential predators, and walked out in a shuffling saunter.

Luke lay on his bed and let each can welcome him. He played his game: which caught his attention first this time? which made his eyes linger longest? what associations did each bring to mind? The new Jolt made him wince at its red and brown ugliness, like the colors for an underfunded inner city sports team. The old Coke brought nostalgia. Long-haired people in bell bottoms, a stadium full, waving lit candles and singing about buying the world a Coke, about teaching the world to sing in perfect harmony about Coke, about Coke adds life! and about the Real Thing. Luke started to cry.

Into his slim, bare pillow, Luke cried, heaving, gasping, choking, strangled, and working up to a tumultuous pitch that he was sure would rattle the cans and cause them to all come crashing down on him to bury him alive. When his fit subsided he was surprised to find only a mild-mannered smear of tears and snot marking the spot where he'd pressed his face.

The attack left him giddy and restless, cagey. The room was now as dark as it would get in the city. He bounced on the squeaking bed, sitting lotus style for a while and then, worried that the other inmates might suspect him of masturbation, he went out.

He blinked at the streetlights and headlights and neon signs as if having emerged from a cave. If any reference to Plato entered his mind, it didn't settle. The Bev was teeming with its Saturday night crowd. Luke found Deirdre at the back, playing pool with her boyfriend on a rare night off.

"I have to talk to you," he said, louder than he'd intended.

She nodded, made her shot, sinking two balls, and, laughing with an easy pride, handed her cue to her boyfriend. The boyfriend eyed Luke warily but then was distracted by bids for Deirdre's cue.

Wavering between clots of people and tossing off greetings here and there, Deirdre led Luke out the side door and into the alley. She leaned against the wall, "What did you want to talk about?"

He didn't know. The interruption of the pool game, the trip outside, her devoted attention, it all seemed to demand something grand and dramatic, it all made him feel stupid. In an attempt to match the circumstances, he said, "I want to get rid of my cans. All of them. Together. I don't want them to be split up. Or recycled. I thought you might know what to do. I thought I might give them all to you."

"Oh Luke," Deirdre slapped the heel of her hand against her forehead sloppily, "I don't want your cans. When are you going to get it? You don't need to give me those cans for me to like you. You don't need those cans to make you special. You're a nice guy. A bit out of it, but nice."

It was Deirdre who didn't get it, Luke thought. It had never occurred to him that his cans might get him liked or noticed. That wasn't the point at all. He wasn't sure what the point was, but he was sure that that wasn't it. He started gently toeing the wall in frustration. "Well, what am I going to do with them? You don't understand. I have to get rid of them."

Deirdre thought for a minute. "I don't know, maybe my prof would want them for something. With the urban myths I've been collecting for her and the photos of old ads painted on buildings we archived, maybe we could do some kind of display, a mini-museum of pop culture or something. I'll have to ask. Why don't you come over for dinner with me and Ben some night and we'll talk about it?"

Luke started. An invitation. He hadn't had one since those grade school birthday parties where the parents invite the whole class. This meant many meetings in preparation. Getting her address, setting a time and day, asking her what he could do, didn't people bring things to dinner or something? He would have to shop for a gift.

"That's a really good idea. Thanks, Deirdre, thanks. I mean it. That would be great." A smile jumped up on his face and he swiped awkwardly at Deirdre's shoulder.

Deirdre gracefully slapped him on the back and said, "Forget about it, it's no problem, really. I've got to get back to Ben. You take it easy. It'll all work out somehow."

He opened the door for her and watched her weave her way back into the throng. Then he ran home and sat on his bed staring at the bottle on the dresser. He climbed into bed with his clothes still on. He peeled off a grey worksock and put the bottle in it. Then he lay down with it, hugging it against his chest. He fell asleep and dreamt of red-winged, bushy-haired angels singing, "YOU LIKE IT, IT LIKES YOU!"

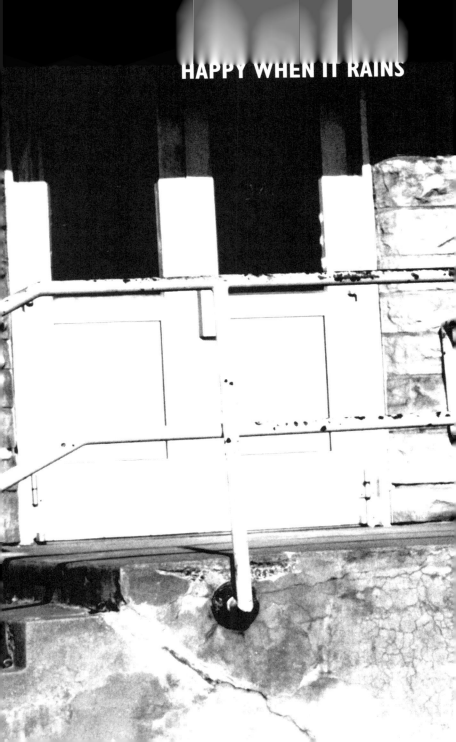

HAPPY WHEN IT RAINS

Cold rain. Hospital green. Brown paint peeling off window frame. Your battered old suitcases nailed to the wall. Open, used as shelves. Books and jars of marbles, pebbles from the Spit in murky water. Chill of spring. The crisscross of milkcrate welts patterning my ass. It was another time we were trying to crawl into, crawling into the bottles, the smoke, the closet we slept in. Playing Jesus and Mary Chain, the Fall, Stiff Little Fingers. Everything smelling like basements, dumpsters, the buy-by-the-pound. Dust and mould flavoring our skin hair breath.

Trying to get clean, to get somewhere new, I ran into the rain and climbed on someone's van all flailing marionette limbs in the rain that smelled of sewers, of subways, of all kinds of subterranean loneliness. I didn't know anyone was in there until they started banging up under my feet and you came to the door and yelled at me to leave them alone. I didn't even know they were there. I wasn't trying to bother anyone.

And it was like that. Any time I tried to get someplace new I was bothering everyone. Something so wordless and sharp whirred in me, pinwheel, propeller, and you were maybe afraid it would cut your slow gentle fingers off, cut you off.

With you everything slowed until it wasn't time at all but something else entirely, another kind of thing, dim and shadowy and damp, like being my own reflection in a puddle.

Lying around all day chainsmoking and reading poetry and touching tender and light. Not even the rain having such small hands as you and I. Yours solid feathers that could make things levitate. Mine decorative appendages that fumbled and dropped everything. Entwined, our hands made wells, baskets, houses, things that could hold, contain, carry, keep safe.

In the old hotel slated for demolition we found bottles and crates from a time when it was important that things lasted, all grimy and sturdy, a stubby beer bottle bringing back being at the knee of someone, old alphabet blocks. We were always finding things we couldn't do anything with. The alphabet blocks spelling out OFUK on the kitchen table crate for weeks.

My belly all bagpipe, I'd have to wait till the King's Flame Diner opened to go to the bathroom because your toilet was broken, your bathtub filled with dirty broken dishes, the kitchen sink disconnected because someone thought it was in the way. Then you were banned from the King's Flame for something, you didn't remember what, being drunk at the time you did it, and drunk at the time I asked about it, and the motherly waitress abandoned me, guilt by association, she wouldn't let me use the washroom any more unless I bought something first. Hair stringy matted, skin zitty and ashen, legs all bruised and the bottoms of my feet stained black. I was more and more turning into something less pretty, something you could know.

Sleeping on the floor of the closet, nesting naked shiver in the old hotel drapes with their anxious geometrics of greens and blues and purples, I'd wake to draw maps of your chest hair on empty cigarette packages and you would have inked sharp petalled roses on my skin to freckle my thighs while I slept.

The time I woke late into trouble, having slept in garters and stockings, putting on top and skirt then finding underwear and putting it on last. Everyone staring at me on the subway but saying nothing. They were putting up a carnival in the shopping mall parking lot as I walked by, all the men stopping work, dropping everything, coming to the yellow barricades between us like seagulls as the hot dog vendor wheeled by, whistling and hooting and saying words I forced my mind to break down into abstract syllables. Gauntlet run, I really didn't think I was as attractive as all that, I really didn't fear myself in that way before, I got to work at the wine store and your friend told me to go look in the mirror, now turn around. The bottom of my skirt had caught in the waistband of my panties at the back. I had been walking around exposing my underwear and garters all over town. And no-one told me. I thought of the women at the bus stop, how they wouldn't meet my eyes. I thought of you sitting up in bed to kiss me good-bye, have a nice day at work. I had turned and walked away from you to work but you hadn't said a word. I'd always assumed you watched me go out. I thought you stared after me just for a New York minute at least as I left you.

And this is the way the story of us goes. There is no reason for it so no beginning. Nothing really happens. No this happened then that happened. No this caused that. Just the rain drumming on itself and the sun not making sense any more and us touching through the dust on each other. And then an ending. At least it has that. Every story has an ending if nothing else.

You sat drunk in the alley as the others broke bottles and threw Ramen noodles inside, you sat drunk in the alley and I slid and plunked drunk onto you in your lap and you were crying. I asked you why. You said: because I'm an asshole and I am going to hurt you, I know I am going to end up hurting you. And I said: you can't hurt me even if you tried, I've been hurt enough that you would be a pinprick, nothing more. And it was true in a way but in another way it wasn't true at all. Sometimes a pinprick hurts worse. Sometimes a pinprick is all it takes. Sometimes it's like that no matter how thick your skin. It's a matter of pressure maybe. Like that balloon trick where the magician sticks the needle in and it is amazing that nothing happens. Until you take the needle out. And everything busts big like hell and shocking. Busts into nothing, a rubbery rag you can't use for anything.

You said you needed some time. Needed some space.

Needed such huge things as that, whole dimensions. I said okay and meant okay because I was okay. I gave you that, what you wanted, but you didn't take it, crawling through my window always at three or four A.M., that being maybe your last minute. Then you broke up with me to keep yourself from coming to my window. You were worried that I'd take you out, I guess, that we would go out, really. Out into all those dimensions you couldn't deal with.

After you broke up with me I went out and let somebody fuck me. And the next night another body. And the next night another. They were all friends with each other and I was hoping they'd compare notes and I would hear about it. I was hoping this because I'd been a different person with each one and I wanted to find out which person it was better to be since being me wasn't working. It hurt a bit. But what hurt more was when I told you about it, because you asked, and you didn't respond at all. Being so very busy staring into the red wine I'd spilled on the acid green linoleum. Being so very busy trying to be nothing to me. Being so very busy trying to be nothing at all.

THE RED MOON

Kay gave the heavy jug of red wine a lingering kiss good-bye. The Ravi Shankar record plucked at matted strings of nerves. Zoe told her mother to fuck off again. Kay wished he could shut her up. He loved her mother. Ever since the time he lived with them as Zoe's first love he was always welcome to have chili or crash there. Even when Zoe wasn't staying there or was off on a rant, he would drop by to shoot the shit with her mother Bee. This bugged the hell out of Zoe. The time Bee told her that Kay had 'good vibes', Zoe went right out to dump him again.

What he saw there was not what Zoe saw there. Kay saw home in the nest of Indian print fabric and macramé. Zoe saw a house owned by her mother, who might either kick her out or try to hold her there, depending on the mood of the moment. Kay heard love in Bee's voice. Zoe heard an ever-changing lie because whatever Bee said she'd contradict her-self in word or action, given time. The lie Zoe heard tonight was the Be Here Now lie.

Zoe had been arguing for the meaninglessness of existence. The basis of her argument was that there was no point in doing anything. You send food to starving children in Bangladesh and then the world is over-populated. You get a job like Bee, work-ing with immigrant women, and then you are stuck paying taxes that support an oppressive government. You buy almost anything, dental floss, whatever, and are unknowingly con-tributing to the depletion of the rain forest, or the exploitation of workers, or genocides, or dictatorships.

Bee said, "You have to trust that the smaller differences add up to larger changes. You are thinking in terms of an ideal future that is never here. You have to live in the moment, appreciating the oneness of all life, to see that the point is in the process and not the end result. You have to Be Here Now, Zoe."

Zoe said, "Be Here Now? Here sucks! Now sucks! Every-

Zoe lit Kay cigarettes as he kept his eyes on the road. He smoked Winstons and the smell was like a spell. It was just as it was before and before and before. The lights and walls rushing past as they sat facing the same direction with smoke and darkness and silence filling the cold space between them as their cigarettes began to flare in unison. Immune behind the frosting glass, moving through mazes in random circular patterns, they sat facing the same direction that was no direction at all really. Without words, signs towards other signs, they sat in the same place that was no place at all really.

Kay braked at a dead-end. The headlights were blocked by a yellow guardrail. "Do you want to walk on the beach or is it too cold?"

"Well, it is too cold but I want to anyway." Zoe tucked her teased black bob under a gray beret and pulled it down over all the rings in her ears. They slammed the van doors and walked through the park. A thin veil of snow shrouded the shore, stained at the edges by the inky waves. Kay strode by the water, his pale skin and bleached hair rising astral from his dark tattered overcoat. Zoe shook behind him, letting his tall body break the wind that whipped the hat down from her head and the white crinoline up from her torn black stockings.

Meditating on Kay's breakwall back, Zoe remembered their engagement. He had asked for her hand and she had said no. She saw her hand severed and bloody, a useless blossom of five petals trailing twisted roots, carried away by him, and she had said no. He never asked for any part of her again and then they were friends. She did not know that she could give her parts and keep her whole, she could give her whole and keep all her parts. She knew only that her parts would be taken, would be taken apart, and then would be left to her for reassembling. She would fill this whole again and then it would be broken open.

The wind died down a bit as they rounded into an inlet. Zoe swirled around Kay, racing past him into the fading howling with her head down. She ran out to the pier and along its flat-footed concrete until she stopped halfway. She stopped halfway in awe of it. It was big and red and round like an enormous egg bursting with blood.

"Holy shit," Kay caught his breath at her side, "that can't be the moon."

The cold stung out water from their eyes, making the moon waver, making it seem to pulse like some immense spherical heart pulsing an expansive and unsteady beat, making them think of love.

Zoe thought of the time they played Pente in the nude with the blue foam of Super Blondissima stacked sloppily on their heads, how they looked like twin ghouls, and how she didn't care with him about how ugly she looked like that.

Kay thought of the time he'd broken into tears when he wasn't invited to either his dad's or his mom's for Christmas, how he'd bawled like a big baby and Zoe had curled around him and squeezed it all out of him, squeezing out even his shame for crying at all.

And in this thinking of love's past, in the presence of such a sign, they were helpless before the possibility of love's future.

Zoe imagining his hand on her belly, her belly all swollen like the moon and her skin belonging to her but stretching between the heat of a small kick inside and the warm barnacle of Kay's hand outside.

Kay imagining her hand entwined with his, both hands all withered and rust-spotted, curling yellow string beans, her hand still playing the hand game with teasing, restless fingers and his hand able to catch hers and contain it for a sharp flash of sweet.

All of this thinking of past and future conjured the presence of love, and suddenly Zoe could smell the sour cream, musky caramel and seashell scent of the back of his neck and Kay could feel the thermal waves roll off her, shivering towards him as her body always seems to give off more warmth than any other. Silence drew him nearer to her as she widened eyes and mouth and then the silence was abruptly interrupted by a near distant voice shouting at them to fuck off.

They turned towards the end of the pier to see the huge flapping raven wings of coats covering two people fucking. Flinching back with the embarrassment of intruders, Zoe and Kay stumbled awkwardly back to the shore. Bowed, they shuffled along the sand separately, Zoe along the water and Kay under the trees, as the wind blew them back to the van. Never looking back at the same time, they twisted their necks over hunched shoulders to see the red moon breaking through shifty clouds and disappearing again.

SANCTUARY

Poppy's stomach is rumbling. Rubbery. So is the subway train she is on. Louder. Less rubbery. As she listens to these rumblings she rummages through her purple sports bag and tugs out a ball of crinkly red cotton. She shakes it out and it scatters little jangling sounds around her. An old peasant skirt, cut short and sewn with tiny Indian bells to make it too heavy for any crime of levity committed by a passing wind. She shrugs off her lumber jacket, with the skirt spread over her lap. Then she bends down and sticks her sneakers into the circle of the skirt, pulling its rustle up to her knees. Just as she is standing to fasten the waistband above that of her jeans, the train screeches into the next station and stops more abruptly than she anticipated. A hula swivel of her hips wobbles her legs with a shower of tinkling clinks, but ultimately preserves her balance, and she takes advantage of this full stop to reach up under the skirt, undo the buttons on her Levis and shimmy them over her black tights down to her ankles. The train starts again and she is thrown back into her seat. Her bag falls to the scuffed floor with a muffled jingle of buried objects.

Maybe it is this jolt or maybe it is the frantic urging of the bells that makes her move more quickly. In any case, she manages to tear off her blue sweater and reveal her bustier for only half a second before wriggling into a red sweatshirt. Which has also been cut short and ringed with bells along the bottom, a vocal few teasing her bellybutton as she bends again to yank off her sneakers and wrestle the jeans onto the floor. By the next screech and stop, she is fully dressed, even down to her toes, which have been squeakingly swallowed by patent leather combats.

She has two more stops to complete the next step of her tintinnabulatory transformation. She shakes a long bellydancer's belt out of the bag and snakes it around her hips. From the delicate weaving of chains hang a crowded gallows of little toys. The kind you can get in machines at the supermarket, where a chicken spins around until its scratchy mechanical clucks announce an egg popping down the silver chute to a small trap door. Cracking these eggs open, Poppy has collected miniature skeletons, glow-in-the-dark cockroaches, faux-diamond rings, pink plastic hearts and much-coveted bloody teeth. All of which, and more, she has hung on her belt to encircle herself with a protective chatter of kitsch.

At the next station, she plops a bandana bundle into her lap and carefully unties the corners. She untangles her mother's old seed bead necklaces and flips them over her head. Then she threads hoops through all of the stretching punctures in her ears, except the lobe ones which receive chiming silver chandeliers. Finally, she slips on bangles up to her elbows. She has to unbutton the sleeves on her lumber jacket to fit her laden wrists through. She picks up her bandana and ties it around her head. Then she undoes the long blonde braid of hair behind her back. When she shakes her head she sounds like a distant bicycle accident. When she dashes out the subway at Queen, banging her bag against the closing doors, she sounds like a distant train wreck.

Poppy knows that dressing like a gypsy doesn't make her a gypsy. Gypsies are people who don't want a home.

At home, Poppy wears moccasins or sneakers. But this doesn't help. Her mother says in a firm, compassionate voice, "Poppy, I'd like to talk to you about the way you walk. You see, you step with your heel first. Stomp, stomp, stomp down the hall. I wonder if you are aware of this because it is very disturbing for the other members of the household."

At home Poppy mostly stays in her room and reads. She doesn't watch her television or play her stereo. She listened to a Walkman for a while, but no matter how low she turned the volume, her mother could hear it anywhere in the apartment. Her mother prides herself on her supersonic hearing abilities, which have been tested by experts and proven to be quite above average. Her mother works as a psychiatric nurse and so also has an above average need for peace and quiet when she returns from bedlam every day.

However, it is only since she hit puberty, crashed right into it, that Poppy has clashed with her mother's supersonic hearing abilities. Since she was thirteen, Poppy has been gradually learning the finer techniques of silence. Not merely refraining from tapping feet or rapping fingers. Not simply modifying a subdued voice to a faint whisper. But twisting doorknobs quietly and easing doors open. Sinking dishes into crisping mounds of soap bubbles. Using a soft toothbrush slowly to be almost inaudible when brushing her teeth. All of these things she has practiced. But some things cannot be muted. Peeing. Chewing. Swallowing. Or muted enough. Stomach growling. Burping. Breathing. In trying to breathe softly she has developed the habit of hyperventilation and is often dizzy.

Inevitably, her mother's voice would become a sharp bark. "For godsake, why can't you be quiet? Why can't you give me a moment's peace?"

Poppy has also learned the art of selective hearing. While she gets quieter and quieter, her mother yells louder and louder for some peace from her. And as her mother yells, Poppy listens for other sounds in the apartment, sounds that don't originate in either Poppy or her mother. The hum of the refrigerator, leaves from a large plant slapping together over the heating vent, her mother's boyfriend singing 'Suzy Q' in the shower. Her mother yells louder, "Selfish, ungrateful little bitch!" and Poppy gets quieter until her mother tries to shake all the hidden noises out of her.

These are the noises that won't give her mother peace, that can't be muted, that Poppy herself can't hear. The noises of Poppy's small breasts bobbing, of her curls of underarm and pubic hair rustling, of her blood splurting onto sanitary napkins. Of incendiary chemicals pumping paths of fire in Poppy's body. But no matter how hard she tries, Poppy's mother can't shake these noises out of Poppy. And so she releases her and tells her to get out of her house.

If the silence she practices could make Poppy disappear completely, she would hang on to it with all of her strong, silent might. But it doesn't make her disappear. She is still there in the apartment. She is still there in the elevator. She is still there on the street. The silence only makes her disappear to others, makes her a shadow where others are light beams darting across each other's paths.

If the silence she practices could make Poppy at peace inside, she would clutch it all around her and nestle down. But it doesn't make her at peace. Quite the contrary. It enlarges all of her thoughts so that they collide in cacophony. The tighter she laces her body into silence, the more furiously her thoughts burst into each other.

Poppy greets the bouncer by name and he opens the door of the Twilight Zone to her. She enters a monstrous metallic heartbeat as the cashier calls shrilly behind her to the bouncer, "What are you doing? She didn't show ID. She didn't pay cover. I told you last time she was..."

Poppy instantly clangors to the women's washroom where, amid the flushings and pourings of water, she holds court for a bevy of black-clad Goth girls and pseudo-skins. Her royalty is supported by three qualifications. One is that nobody else dresses like Poppy. Although imitators have recently begun a procession of that form of flattery at her high school. Which irritates Poppy to no end. Especially because there is now talk of dress regulations that would ban distractingly noisy styles of apparel.

The next qualification is that, in contrast to her clamourous costume, Poppy rarely speaks. This is seen not as a subdued mousiness but as a sign of superiority, contempt, disdain. Poppy is simply above the exuberant chatter of rumour, even when the rumours are about her. She is above them. She is above everything. Worrying about grades, boyfriends, social status, making curfew. She is above being concerned about anything at all. She will jingle and jangle her way through life unaffected by anything. A paragon of the new virginity, the heart that will never be handled, the lips that will never curl up at the corners and open.

She is not a paragon of the old virginity. Everybody knows that Poppy has slept with everybody. And also that she has sex silently, coolly, as if a dry silk sheet was drifting over her. And that she doesn't give out her phone number, never mind waiting for his call. For this reason, she is pursued for extended periods of time.

What everybody doesn't know is that Poppy doesn't even know why she allows these boys to have sex with her, even sometimes when it doesn't provide her with a place to sleep. She doesn't particularly enjoy it. But listening to their noises, their choo-choo puffs of breath and god-jesus-christ babble and final deep burst of oh! hollows her head into a churchly echo chamber and she finds comfort in this. And most of the time it does provide her with a place to sleep: the middle-class crisp sheets of beds belonging to parents on holiday at Club Med, the shabby squeaking sheetless box springs belonging to boys who quit school to wash dishes, the crunchy crumb-filled futons on the floor belonging to hard-core punk musicians.

For there is one thing and one thing only that worries Poppy, and that is a place to sleep. For she can never predict when her mother will bark or howl an eviction notice. While she takes secret pleasure in the cool high song of arrogance her where sucks! Being here now for you means living in your own home with food and money. Being here now for me means being evicted from dumps and eating Kraft dinner while wasting my time working shit jobs making money for assholes. You fucking hippies got all the money, all the jobs, all the houses, all the sex, and we are just left paying for it all. Be here now, fuck off! I mean FUCK OFF!"

Now he would have to drive Zoe to her apartment because she had told Bee to fuck off. Another Thanksgiving with no thanks given. Bee gave him a quick hug as he trailed Zoe's warrior path out the door. He searched his pockets for his car keys, the crashes of Bee's breaking of bric-a-brac interrupting the sitar music as if a trance dancer had fallen on a drum set. He wanted to get away before Bee started crying but he couldn't find the damn keys.

Zoe leaned against the pirate flag painted on his VW van with her arms folded across all the zippers on her jacket. She stretched two fists in front of her and called, "Which hand?" He came down and picked the left and found his keys. She said, "I don't know what you do without me," and they got into the van.

"Where are you living now?" He warmed up the engine.

"It doesn't matter. I don't want to go there. Just drive around, okay?"

It was very late and he swerved wildly around corners, careening up and down alleys and doing doughnuts in parking lots. They sped through the financial district with a light snow falling from a sky they couldn't see. No signs of life, only empty lights speckling this tunnel up to its impossibly high ceiling. He zigzagged across the left and right lanes. Zoe felt perfectly safe. Except for the odd taxi, they were alone on the road. And he had taken a stunt-driving course after the guitar lessons and before the welding certificate.

social position surrounds her with, she knows the real noise. The rusty grating of her mother's voice, the raucous raccoon laughter of her mother's boyfriend, the remembered giddy racket of her childhood giggles, the thin whine of her secret self-pity, the manic madrigal of her strategies for survival. Her strategy for this night is to sell a lot of bennies.

This is the third qualification of her popularity: Poppy sells pink hearts, robin's eggs and black beauties. These are caffeine pills sold in the back pages of magazines like Cosmopolitan to Americans as diet aids. Poppy has them sent to an old camp friend in New York, who then mails them to Poppy in Toronto. One hundred tabs cost $14.95, plus shipping and handling. Poppy sells them for fifty cents or a dollar each and pulls in about forty dollars a weekend, depending on her own use. This doesn't provide her with a place to sleep because even the crusty fly-spattered rooms at the Spadina Hotel cost at least forty dollars a night. But if she takes some of the pills at regular intervals, she can stay up all night for three days, and if she sells enough she has the money for late-night restaurants like Just Desserts and Fran's. Usually after three days she can go back to her mother's apartment and her mother will seem to have forgotten everything.

Sometimes, she takes too many and they put her to sleep. Especially if she expends a lot of energy creating a din on the dancefloor. This is one of those occasions.

Poppy is curled, or furled, on her side in a corner of the black club where the beat-driven lights can barely tap her. She is snoring lightly, a purr of surf, not enough to wake herself up. She is awakened by the gentle ringing of the bells above her belly. She is aware that she hasn't moved. And so she hasn't caused this minor rippling of small tin hands clapping, which resounds softly in the hush of light, light no longer choreographed by any industrial electronic cacophony. In this hush, she hears also the subtle furry slide of skin on sateen. She opens her eyes to see one of her breasts larger than it should be. And lumpy. There is a hand on her breast, underneath the sweatshirt, stroking her bustier.

The bouncer leans over her, saying, "I left the lights on."

She rolls onto her back and reaches up with one hand to rub the stubble on his head, taking dreamy pleasure in the bristly sound of this motion, like the sound of peeling bandaids off cheap velvet. He takes her hand and she closes her eyes, hearing the wet slap of his tongue against her palm.

She is still pressing her ear down on the left side of his chest, his heartbeat plodding now through the drudgery of slumber. He is wheezing in his sleep, a tickly rippling of wind, a thumb running along the teeth of a comb. The beat flutters and flaps. His breath begins a rasping staccato sawing, slicing into the surrounding oxygen uselessly. His face turns a synthesizer high-C note of blue. Poppy pounds his chest with her rattle-wristed fists. She clutches his shoulders and shakes him, shaking herself to shake him. His eyes still closed, he grabs her arms and throws her off, springing to a sitting position and coughing deeply and hoarsely. She scrabbles into his motorcycle jacket and busily unzips pockets until she finds his inhaler. She hands it to him. As he huffs, she hands him some robin's eggs and gets dressed in a hurried, even furied, flurry.

Standing, she bends to brush dust from her stockings and hoist her bag over her shoulder. "Are you going to be okay?"

Still huffing, he nods.

She pauses, tapping the toe of her left boot onto the right. "Well... see ya."

His head still bent over the inhaler, he raises his hand and waves. She clangors out.

In the phone booth she plucks out the earphones of her Walkman, listens to the coin clatter down, and beeps the number in. The band Fear growls from the dangling earphones: "I seen an old man have a heart attack in Manhattan. He died while we just stood there looking at him — ain't he cute? I don't care about you — FUCK YOU! I don't care about you — FUCK YOU!" Poppy is tapping her only long fingernail against the handle of the receiver in time to the trills echoing the ringing that must be singing through her best friend's house, quietly counting, "One, two, three, four..."

A loud voice bellows, "What!"

"It's me, Poppy," a hesitant scrawl of a voice.

"Are you out again?"

"Yeah."

"Meet me at the Fiesta in half an hour."

"Okay."

Frannie hangs up first.

The lead singer is now blustering: "I've seen men rolling drunks, bodies in the street, a man who was sleeping in his puke, and a man with no legs..." Poppy slips the earphones into her ears again. She starts walking up Yonge Street. Saturday crowds stare at her noise, turn back, stare again. She strides on, weaving and bobbing through clumps of cackling shoppers, their clucking tongues mere accompaniment for the snorts and sprays of traffic stampeding through remaining slush. A new Fear song comes on:

> *My house smells just like a zoo*
> *It's chock full of shit and puke*
> *Got roaches on the walls*
> *Crabs are crawling on my balls*

O but I'm so clean-cut
I just want to fuck some slut
O I love living in the city
I love living in the city

Spent my whole life living in the city
Where junk is cheap
And the air smells shitty
People puking everywhere
Eyes of blood and scabs of hair
Bodies wasted in the heat
People dying in the streets
All the scumbags, they don't care
They just get fat and dye their hair

This is the soundtrack for the movie of her life. At this moment and at others. With this soundtrack framing her scene, the street is not just a busy street, the city is not just a crowded city. The street is her street. The city is her city. And the silence that sucks all of what she hears and sees into a mundane meaninglessness is shaken and shattered until it splits wide open, revealing all of the sounds that it conceals. Sounds of pain and rage and fear. Sounds of pain and rage and fear laughing at themselves.

Poppy laughs little and sweet when she feels a tug on the tail of her lumber jacket. She yanks out her earphones and twirls clinking around. A boy her height, not tall, stands there with his lower lip hanging and a long, long, long strand of drool stretching down to the toe of his left Doc. He bends to break it and blubber it loose from his lip.

"Hey, Poppy."

"Hey, what's up?"

"Can you get me some more glue?" he points to Mr. Gameway's Ark across the street and crumples some worn bills into her hand.

"Why can't you get it?"

"They won't sell it to me any more. Assholes."

"Yeah, okay."

"Here, I'll watch your bag while you go in."

"Yeah right. Fuck you, Jimbo."

Poppy returns with three tubes in a side pocket of her bag, "Here."

"Where's my change? I get $1.64 back."

"That's my cut."

"What cut? We never agreed on a cut. Don't fuck me, give it here."

"I don't have it."

"What do you mean you don't have it?"

"I don't have any change."

"You don't have any change because you scoffed the glue, right? Well, if you got it free then give me my money back."

"No fucking way. I took the risk, I take the cash."

Poppy starts to turn away but Jim tackles her and brings her noisily to the ground. They are lying across the sidewalk, holding up pedestrians. The curb is supporting Poppy's neck and shoulders and her head is bobbing in the street. She brings her arms up and crosses them under her head, as if listening to birds in a park, one hand still clutching the bills. She listens to the tires swerving away from her and the splatters of grey sludge hitting her face, her hair, Jim's shaved head, and the shoulders of his bright green leather jacket. Cramps green. She looks up at Jim's puffing, feeling his chest expand and contract against hers. Another dribble of drool has slipped over the edge of his lip and is swinging pendulously above her chin.

They stare at each other without speaking, Jim breathing hard. Then Jim says, "Give me my money."

Poppy shakes her head.

"Give me my fucking money!"

Poppy starts whistling.

"Fuck, Poppy. Don't be such a bitch."

"Say please. Say please, Great Goddess Poppy."

"Please-great-goddess-Poppy."

"I didn't hear any capitals."

"What the fuck?"

"You have to say it with capitals — Great Goddess Poppy."

"Okay, fuck, Please Great Goddess Poppy."

The drool is dangerously close to Poppy's chin, "Okay, get off me."

Jim rolls over on his side, watching her warily. Poppy hands him two dollars as she sits up.

"What's this? Two fucking dollars!"

"It's more than you would have got if I'd paid for the glue so don't be such a prick."

Jim scrambles up and takes off to his alley. Poppy picks up her bag and continues up the street, the ends of her hair slapping wetly against the fuzz on her jacket, smelling like the street. Hopefully, Frannie will know of a party tonight and then she can take a bath.

"You smell like a sewer," is the first thing Frannie says, with a slight snort.

Poppy slides into the little red booth, kicking her bag under the table. She takes a paper napkin from its dispenser and wipes the grey off her face.

"Why don't you let me cut that long hair off? It's only a hassle and it's so unhip."

Poppy looks at Frannie's crisp and jagged rooster-red crew-cut. Poppy was the one who had hacked Frannie's hair and dyed it, but she had taken a lot of bennies so it was uneven in an unintentional asylum-inmate fashion. She unscrews the salt shaker and leaves the top on evenly. "Hah, you just want revenge."

Frannie snorts again, more severely, and screws the top back on the salt shaker. The waiter comes and Frannie orders for them, two beers, burgers and fries.

"Any parties this weekend?"

"You didn't go to school, did you?"

"Not Thursday and Friday."

"If you went to school you would know. I'm not going to reinforce your nefarious absenteeism by telling you now. Besides, I've got someplace better for us to go."

Poppy stayed at Frannie's house once and she hated it. The family kept jumping up to bring different reference books to the table and debate the correct meaning of terms with warring dictionaries in the midst of heated discussion. Which is one of the reasons Poppy doesn't stay there when her mother kicks her out. The other is that Frannie shares a small room with her two younger sisters.

Frannie is waiting for Poppy to ask her where they have to go. Frannie doesn't believe that someone is paying attention to her unless they are talking back to her as loudly and dramatically as she talks. Poppy envies the ease with which Frannie plays up required adolescent posturing. Poppy is taking pleasure in rolling and tapping her knuckles across the table's imaginary piano keys. Poppy is taking pleasure in not asking Frannie where they have to go.

"Well?"

"Well, what."

Frannie bangs her fist on the table and leans forward to screech, "Well, aren't you going to ask me where we are going?"

"Okay," Poppy keeps up her rapping on the table.

"Okay, what?" Frannie is almost screaming now and heads

are turning.

"Okay, where?" Poppy is nonchalant.

Frannie bangs her fist again, "Sanctuary! That's where."

For a second, the two glare slightly to the right of each other's heads in silence. Then Poppy scrunches up her round flat face. "Is that a new club?"

"No, Jingles. I'm talking about my brother's apartment. He left for a conference in New York today and he's allowing me temporary residence. And I'm offering you sanctuary there so don't be such a shit." Frannie makes a disgusted *shkah* noise at the back of her throat.

Poppy tries to make the same noise back in mockery but can't quite get it. The more tries she makes, the more choked and spluttering she becomes, until Frannie has to stand up in her seat and bend over to pound her on the back, with a vigour that demonstrates her pleasure in this task.

"Sorry," Poppy says, gulping air.

Poppy and Frannie shuffle back down Yonge Street arm in arm, their faces slapping and flapping against the sharp spring wind. It's the comparatively tranquil twilight between Saturday shopping hours and the time when taxis can choose their customers. Poppy and Frannie are not tranquil. Poppy is carrying Frannie's bag and Frannie is carrying Poppy's and they have Poppy's Walkman between them with the right earphone in Poppy's ear and the left in Frannie's, forcing them to lean towards each other. They are listening to X. And singing, or shrieking, along.

> *Every other week I need a new address*
> *Landlord landlord landlord clean up the mess*
> *My whole fucking life is a wreck*

We're desperate — get used to it
We're desperate — get used to it
We're desperate — get used to it
It's just like hellllll...

Crossing Wellesley, they slip on what must be the last patch of ice in Toronto, the earphones popping out of their ears and the Walkman smashing on the curb a foot ahead of them as they crash down and sprawl across the street. Frannie sits up first and checks for cars. None coming. She sings the next line of the song. "Last night everything broke!" and the two collapse in giggles, Poppy's jewelry giggling with them.

Frannie opens the door to number 668 and flicks on the light, announcing."Our Sanctuary — The Neighbour of the Beast."

She walks straight to the bathroom and begins drawing a bath for Poppy. The gurgling and splurting of the tapwater fills the almost empty one-room apartment. Poppy thuds down her bag and the box of M&M packages she's just boosted from a delivery truck. She looks around, unimpressed. It is the prototype middle-class first apartment. In the middle of the parquet floor is a fluffy white duvet over a thick fresh futon. At one corner of this bed is a large new TV and a stereo, obviously parental house-warming gifts. The only other furniture is a matte black Ikea computer desk with matching chair. Books and files line wall shelves above it. Poppy stomps her wet boots into the kitchenette and peeks into the cupboards. There are only two of everything. But the mugs, plates and bowls all match. Frannie comes back from the bathroom and starts to unroll a couple of fifties shirtwaist dresses from her bag and hang them in the closet next to a few button-down shirts. Poppy watches this from the kitchen until she can hear the jet of water growing less urgent in its propulsion as the level of the water rises to the spout.

Poppy drops all of her jewelry and her belt clamourously onto the tiled floor. The sounds rebound off the walls. She lets her clothes fall unto the heap of metal and climbs into the lukewarm bath. Frannie yells from the closet, "Oooeee, guess what I found!"

Quickly, seizing the opportunity to correct her previous refusal to respond, Poppy calls back, "What?", grateful to have decided against a shower. Pleased with the resonance of her light voice in the closed moist air, she continues calling, "What. What-what. What-what-what…"

Frannie presses her forehead against the bathroom door and rattles the knob. Locked. She screams against it, "How can I tell you if you don't fucking shut up? Poppy!"

Poppy keeps chanting under her breath. The whats have begun to sound like twats.

Frannie says, "Bushmills! Forty ounces!"

Poppy interrupts her chant to make gagging noises but Frannie has moved away from the door. She sinks the lower half of her face under water and starts blowing bubbles.

When she emerges from the bathroom, fully dressed with her hair in sopping braids, Frannie is out having a cigarette on the balcony. Poppy joins her.

"What are you doing out here with wet hair?"

"Well, you said we can't smoke inside. What else am I supposed to do?"

They lean over the balcony and look into the parking lot below, which is right beside Comrades, a gay club that doesn't allow women in. They've tried to get in with some of their gay male friends, but Frannie's large breasts gave them away. The Eurythmics are playing at a high volume.

Frannie says, "Comrades is going to get busted if they keep

the music that loud."

Poppy says, "That's not the club, it's coming from the balcony above us."

They lean out further and twist their torsos around to look up. They see two sets of hands curled around the bottoms of two glasses. This vantage point makes them laugh. Two stubbly chins emerge and then they are staring up at two guys in starched collars.

The guy with the slicked-back hair calls down, "Hey, girls, you wanna come up to the party?"

Frannie yells up, "No!"

Poppy smiles and asks, "You got any food up there?"

Frannie is saying, "No, Poppy, no."

The guy with a swingy bob says, "Yeah, we got sandwiches, chips," he calls back to people they can't see, "What do you call those things? Crustettes?"

Slick says, "Come on up, we'll feed you."

Frannie snorts. Poppy says, "Nah, I can't come up. Why don't you throw something down?"

She leans out further and opens her mouth wide.

A flat rubbery brown thing sails down, slaps against her cheek, and falls onto a patch of snow below. They are all laughing. Poppy feels something moist smeared on her face. She points her tongue at it. Mustard. Frannie is pointing at the brown thing on the snow, "What the hell is it?"

Slick gasps, "A tongue!" and clutches his buddy who is also bent over.

Poppy asks, "A tongue? What kind of tongue?"

Buddy says, "You know, a cow tongue. From my tongue sandwich."

"Well," Poppy cocks an eyebrow, "Thanks for the tongue-lashing."

Frannie snorts and Poppy goes in to wash her face. Frannie

follows, opening the Bushmills.

They stay up all night, drinking Bushmills and eating M&Ms and watching the Much Music rotation repeat itself. Poppy has never seen Much Music before. It's new. Still, they spend more time looking at the huge poster of Einstein on the wall than at the screen. Frannie has abandoned her smoking-on-the-balcony rule and the kissing noises of their drags punctuate the videos. They lie silent, smoking and feeling slightly sick to their stomachs, relieved to not be thinking about anything at all, utterly depleted of energy. Until the new Madonna video comes on again. Then they leap up and mimic the actions of the back-up singers, singing, "True Blue, baby, I love you," in deliberately squeaky voices. When it ends, they lie down again, muttering, "Stupid trashy pop-tart. Running bitch of capitalism. She's so fucking fake," and waiting for it to come on again.

They sleep all day and then Frannie leaves to have dinner with her family, one of the conditions of her being allowed to stay at her brother's over March break at school. This becomes their routine: up all night, sleep all day, Frannie leaving and coming back. While Frannie is gone, Poppy is trapped in the apartment without a key. Poppy would probably just stay in the apartment anyway. After the first night, Poppy went to go to the store before Frannie had to leave and Frannie asked her, "Are you sure you have the key? You have your wallet? Aren't you going to button your jacket up?" Poppy had never been asked these kinds of questions before and it made her strange-ly sad. It also rattled her. All of a sudden, going outside seemed like a perilous journey, requiring all kinds of attention to details that Poppy had never thought about much before.

When she got outside, Poppy felt as if she shouldn't be

there. For the first time she felt self-conscious because of all the noise she made just walking down the street. She felt eyes looking at her from every direction. When she got to the convenience store, she'd lost her nerve and had to pay for the decorating magazines she wanted. At least this way she had a brown paper bag to hide them in. She smuggled them back into the apartment under her jacket and didn't take it off until Frannie had left.

This is what Poppy does when she is alone in the apartment. She looks at decorating magazines and imagines her own home. She only conjures up interiors. Sometimes it is big and white and sweetly blank except for a white grand piano and a white fake-fur rug. The piano is always playing by itself. Sometimes it is small and red and curiously crowded with old dusty furniture that is romped on by yelping dogs and yowling cats and yapping ferrets. Most of the time it is huge and black and frenetically filled with bicycles, noisy dada machines, drumsets, amplifiers. But no matter how she imagines this home, she can never see herself moving through these rooms or their oxygen inhabiting her inhalations and exhalations. They remain empty, their sounds inhuman. Poppy gives up and plays Bauhaus on her Walkman. She lies on her back watching the pulse of shadows and whispering, "I'm dead, I'm dead, I'm dead."

Friday night is their last night in the apartment. It is three A.M. and they are smoking on the balcony, Frannie having re-instated the rule. The air is milder. All of the snow has melted and is panting to sewers everywhere, singing a clear cool splashing song. The tongue below is being carried away. Frannie and Poppy don't notice. Frannie and Poppy are watching two figures in the parking lot. They wouldn't have noticed them there in the shadows if they both weren't whitely bald. The one standing against the wall has a fringe framing his pallid pate. The one kneeling in front of him has a bright green collar ringing the base of his bare bobbing head.

Frannie and Poppy are laughing, not loudly. Not Frannie's somewhat snidely snorting chortles or Poppy's lightly lilting gasps of giggles. A tourist laugh. Not unpleasantly surprised. Attempting politeness. Until Poppy stops first. Frannie follows.

"That looks like Jim's jacket," Frannie says quietly.

"Yeah," whispers Poppy.

They smoke in silence until the man zips up his pants and the boy rises. The man walks away and the boy scrapes his back down the wall to squat, taking something out of his boot and putting it into his pocket, taking out a cigarette and cupping his hands around his face to light it.

Frannie starts singing raucously, "Jimbo, Jimbo, on the Uncle Bobby show..."

Poppy disappears inside, slamming the screen door shut. The boy is walking to their apartment building at the back of the lot. Poppy screeches the door hinges open again and starts wailing along with Frannie. The boy is yelling up, "Who the fuck are you?"

They stop their caterwauling. Poppy yells down, "It's me, Poppy."

"And Frannie."

"Yeah, well, fuck you Frannie and Poppy. Most of all, fuck you Poppy."

Poppy starts singing *Happy Birthday to You* in a false operatic soprano. Then she and Frannie start chucking the remaining M&M packages down at Jimmy. The last one hits him in the forehead. He bends down to pick it up. Poppy has attached a ten dollar bill to it with an elastic hairband from her braid. Frannie and Poppy run back into the apartment, squealing like tires before the crescendo of a car crash, and collide on the bed.

The alarm crows awake and they dress groggily, Poppy in her full regalia. There are empty M&M packages, overflowing ashtrays, and dirty styrofoam cups all over the floor. The bottle of Bushmills is broken on the kitchenette tiles. Boot-tracks circle the apartment. There is a grey ring around the tub. Toothpaste is crusted in spatters on the sink.

Poppy jingles and jangles out to the balcony to have a cigarette. She leaves the door propped open to air the place out. Frannie starts emptying ashtrays, collecting garbage. Poppy comes back in and starts to sweep, skipping and wriggling across the floor. Frannie is scrubbing the bathtub, wincing in time to Poppy's singing, "Skip, skip, skip to the loo."

Poppy's jewelry is making a din with every move she makes and she is making many moves. The clamour has been enlarging for Frannie all week. She has begun grinding her teeth against it. She snorts and throws the sponge across the bathroom. The sponge slaps the wall and slurps down it a bit before smacking onto the floor. She stomps out to Poppy.

"For fuck's sake, Jingles, can't you leave that shit off for one fucking day, just one fucking day so I can have some peace and quiet while I clean up your bloody mess, you bitch."

Poppy stands silent for a minute. She drops the broom, letting it crash down, and takes a deep breath. She starts shrieking the Dead Kennedys' version of *I Fought the Law* and jumping all over the bed, shaking every laden part of her body.

Frannie storms out of the apartment. *Shkah, shkah, shkah.*

Poppy lies down on the bed and catches her breath. Her rage is a commotion that can't be challenged by any real racket. She is listening to the sounds of destruction that would prevail if she struck the TV screen hard with the broom handle, if she smashed the dishes against the window, if she hurled the computer over the balcony.

Too much energy is buzzing through her for her to remain prone. She gets up and starts cleaning vigorously. When it's all done, she paces the balcony, chainsmoking. Eventually, she is interrupted by a voice calling out from the parking lot below. Her attention shifts outside of herself and she pauses her pacing to listen.

"Rapunzel! Rapunzel! Let down your long hair!"

She leans over the balcony. Frannie is standing below, "Didn't you hear me buzz up? I forgot my key!"

Poppy shakes her head.

"Well, let me up now!"

Poppy nods her head, throws her cigarette butt down, and goes in. Frannie's still somewhat withering voice crackles over the intercom and Poppy beeps her in. When she enters the apartment, Poppy is sitting quietly on the edge of the fresh-sheeted futon.

Frannie starts taking her clothes out of the closet, the empty hangers clattering as she packs, "So are you going to take that shit off now?"

Poppy is mute.

"What, you're not talking to me?"

Just the tinkle of Poppy leaning back to lie down.

Frannie goes over to the bed and lies on her stomach beside Poppy. "I wouldn't make such a big deal out of it if it wasn't really getting on my nerves."

They lie silent for some stretching seconds. Then Poppy says, "You remember that party after the Not Dead Yet benefit?"

Frannie shrugs.

"We were sitting on that disgusting yellow couch next to that guy, you know."

"What guy?"

"You know, that passed-out guy. We were next to him practically the whole party."

"What passed-out guy? There's always a passed-out guy on that couch."

"You know, the guy everybody figured was passed out but the next gig we found out that he hadn't been passed out, he was dead."

"Dead?"

"He'd OD'd on junk and nobody realized it until late the next day."

"Oh, yeah, that guy. What was his name?"

"I don't think we ever knew."

"Dave?"

"No, it was one of those chosen names. Scum. Piss. Something obvious like that."

"Well," Frannie gets it and gets up, "maybe he wasn't really dead, maybe it was just a stupid rumour."

"Yeah."

"It's possible though."

"Yeah."

"Hey, let's go out for breakfast."

Poppy rouses herself, "Okay."

The subway rattles and wheezes on. Poppy takes off her boots and slips her jeans on under her skirt and ties on her sneakers. Then she lets the skirt and belt clatter to the floor. She strips off her bracelets and lets them jangle onto her skirt. She plucks out her earrings and tucks them into the pocket of her jeans. She flips off her necklaces, letting them tangle with the bracelets. Shrugging out of her jacket, she bends over her bag and pulls out her sweater. She yanks off her sweatshirt, despite its rings of protest, and wrestles the sweater on. She takes a package out of the bag, places it on her lap, bends again and stuffs all of her clamourous costume in the bag. The giftwrapping on the package is a collage of photographs of disco dancers. A Travolta clone has been cut out and taped on as a card. She can make him stand up, his finger pointing to the train ceiling. She reads his back, "Made these for you. Didn't want to give them to you until you left, for obvious reasons. Love, Frannie."

Poppy rips open the package. There are two strips of red leather with big jinglebells sewn onto them at regular intervals, and a series of fasteners sewn onto the ends so that Poppy can adjust them to the ankles of her boots. Poppy puts them into her bag just as the train pulls into her station and screeches to a stop.

THE NEW PANTS

Window-framed sharkskin sky. Sharp spring wind biting
through the plastic taped to a triangular hole in the
glass pane. Kev is rolling onto his back and scratching
his balls. Scratching what wakes first. Rising to untape the
plastic and pee out the window. Not shaking it out for to do
so would court castration, a bite sharper than that of any wind.
Piss pooling on the window ledge outside then seeping into
the concrete, spare drops dribbling over the edge.

The doorbell is ringing and Kev struggles into his last pair
of jeans, with their rip at the crotch that puts him at risk for
an indecent exposure charge. Kev is peeping through the spy-
hole. Not the bald head of the short, stocky landlord. Kev is
pulling the chain loose from its track, rattling the lock open
and opening the door. Kev is looking up at Patty's new haircut — a brown bob — and Patty is reaching out to grab the
penis drooping out of Kev's jeans, giving it a firm shake, saying, "Hi, how are ya, pleased to meetcha."

Kev is stumbling back, slapping her hand away, and she is
marching in with a briefcase, letting it barely bounce on the
raw foam that Kev sleeps on. Patty is sitting and crossing her
nude-stockinged legs. Sitting on the old plaid armchair, leaning back against the spray paint spelling out 'Mr. Chair' across
the rough fabric. Dust is rising and falling, moth breath. Kev is
bending to open the briefcase, finding glossy travel brochures
and a photocopy of Bugs Bunny advertising Reg Hartt's cartoon revival. On the back, a scrawled outline of all the steps of
their *khat* run to England tomorrow morning.

Quickly, across Kev's inner landscape, a toy plane circling
the ceiling, an empty suit saying, "Bond. James Bond," and his
lips catching dark stars in the constellation of freckles on
Patty's shoulder.

Kev is running his hand through his new short haircut, his
fingers twirling in their surprise at avoiding tangles. Kev is

saying, "I don't know about this, I don't know."

Patty is saying, "Look under the brochures and files. Look."

Kev is letting his fingers do the looking, pulling out a clip-on tie, a button-down striped shirt and tan pants.

Patty is saying, "Try them on, go on."

Kev is laying the clothes out on the foam, first the shirt, then the pants over it so that the shirt looks like it is tucked into the waistband of the pants, then the tie covering the shirt buttons. He is trying to see himself lying on the foam inside of these clothes but he is failing. He sits cross-legged on the floor, absent-mindedly squeezing a zit on the hairy thigh exposed by another tear in his jeans.

Patty lights a cigarette for him. Then one for herself.

Kev is picturing himself in a natty gangster suit, a fedora shadowing his thick-lashed blue eyes, sucking on his cigarette held between the first fingers and the thumb, it tasting first of burnt marshmallows, then of fried bacon, and finally of dank radiator steam. Patty in a tight red dress with a dark marcelled wave framing a white face with a tart cranberry pucker, saying, "How about it, big boy?" and blowing him a cherubic kiss.

Kev is bending over to pick up the shirt and Patty is getting a full view of the dark hairs on his ass frowning over his red-rimmed googly balls. Patty is laughing and Kev is biting his lip as he buttons on his shirt all wrong and reaches for the pants, throwing them over his shoulder as he bends again to unzip and struggle out of his jeans.

Those new pants, what pants they are. A firm waistline, gently pleated, rippling into generous pockets. Bagging with saucy insouciance at the crotch and ass. Narrowing evenly down the legs to the perfect width of crisp, stalwart cuffs. Pants that say Clark Gable, Ernest Hemingway, African safaris, French fishing villages, streamlined curvaceous automobiles. Patty gets a new picture of Kev strolling barefoot on a clean, white beach, blowing his nose into a linen handkerchief, rolling up his sleeves to hurl smooth pebbles into surging ocean swells. Kev saying, "How about it, Patty-pie?" and picking her up to wade them both into the lapping blue water.

Kev does not know what Patty is picturing. Patty does not know what Kev is picturing. And so, in this moment, they do not know each other. For each is only the reach of their respective desires and the frustration of the impossibility of those desires. In this time, between staying and leaving, between the defined past and the indefinite future, between former selves and selves that they will become, they don't even know themselves. They know only that they desire selves, selves that will come to them easily, without the slightest effort beyond the range that their limited purchasing power will allow.

"Those are some fine pants," Patty is whistling, "let's go get a jacket and shoes and then go celebrate your new pants."

Three in the morning and Patty is leaving the dark apartment with a forty-ounce bottle containing only two fingers of scotch. Sighing loudly. And yelling, "I'll pick you up at six and you better be ready, asshole."

Kev is dreaming. Dreaming of Patty the way she looked before this week. Long, thin, green braids. Purple lipstick. Overalls cut into shorts. Black long-johns. Grey work socks with flirtatious red stripes. Patty with yellow teeth and chapped lips, licking his clavicle. Patty squatting to pee on broken glass in the alley behind the bar. Patty shaving her legs in the fountain at Queen and University, her legs bright silver and dorsal in the sprays of light cascading a lacy swath through the darkness.

Kev is dreaming beyond memory, dreaming of a Kev unknown. A Kev in black cowboy boots and hat, lying in the back seat of a black Riviera and drinking Jack Daniels. Patty singing, "I killed a man in Reno just to watch him die," and shooting out the driver's seat window into vulnerable cacti. A Kev in black leather pants straddling a mike stand and howling. Patty butting the neck of a red guitar into his hip. A Kev in a black turtleneck, slouching in a smoky cafe and writing words like "fellatio grin of the moon" in black scrawls across damp napkins. A naked Kev, rolling in black paint across a white-clad Patty and signing his name on her palm.

Kev is dreaming beyond Patty, dreaming of a woman unknown. A woman with bristling red curls and a carnivorous smile. Pouring martinis and plopping olives into them. The spray hitting her sharp cheekbones. Kev drinking martini after martini in the blue velvet lounge. Reaching into the pocket of his plaid suit jacket for change and tossing it like darts into her downy cleavage. Singing, "You are my sunshine..." and swallowing the olives whole. Laying his head down in the ashtray and snoring.

Kev is snoring, he is beyond dreaming. Beyond desire. Beyond his self.

Six in the morning and Patty is pounding on the door. Kicking her suitcase and screaming, "Wake up you fuck, you fucking fuck-up."

Kev is sleeping, fresh vomit on his face, fresh vomit on his new pants.

Kev is dreaming again. Dreaming of fins cleaving through clean water, through fine sand, and through pressed tan fabric up to the crotch.

THE SCRAPBOOK

Buoyant and buzzing with the ions of the storm, he leaps up the leaning steps of the old Victorian house as lightning flashes. Pacing the garbage-piled porch, he sees himself struck, the thin, white flame striking sparks against his teeth as it shoots deep inside him to splice fine nerve wires. He would be plugged in to this wall of night, a circuit box for every electrical undercurrent towing the moon across the sky. The front door is wide open. He runs upstairs, sensing that presence will be possible, that a moment is immanent.

He runs into the back bedroom. He leans against the doorway, shifting creaks of the worn wood planks. He is afraid to step in, afraid he might fall forever, that there is nothing to hold him. The ceiling, the walls, the baseboards, even the floor, are painted a flat black. With the power out, he can't even turn on the overhead light that would map the crowded objects of colour in the room. He waits at the doorway for the next flash, the celestial camera hovering to record each picture of this night. He waits for the next flash to find her in the black room, to find her and hold her in one shadowless moment.

The flash comes but she is not there on the wrought iron bed, she is not there lying on the floor among Mason jars of dead flowers. A breeze blows spray in from the cracked window. It is open.

He goes to close it, for a minute resting his sharp elbows on the puddled sill. He looks out. He sees her then, lying on the broken squares of tar shingles, their sandpaper surface glittering under spits of rain. She is naked under drumming droplets, shivering to the staccato beat. She lifts her head, twisting her neck around as he contorts through the square opening. He crouches, edging his way down to her, heelstep by heelstep so as not to slide down the step. He wonders if this is such a good idea. The old shed below was not used because it leaked so much. He could leak through it. He lifts his face to the sky.

She sits up, hugging her knees to her breasts, feeling the rivulets of rain webbing around her jutting hip and shoulder curves, like a net of external veins. Her black hair slaps his arm as she nestles her head against his neck, looking down at the streaks of darkening colour converging on his t-shirt.

"Wait," she says, "Wait till you see."

The next flash of lightning torches a bonfire of roses in the neighbour's yard. The small glare of grass is entirely circled by full-blown blooms — apoplectic hearts exploding out of labyrinthine mouths, spraying red sparks into the white light. They have seen red before. Now they know it. It feeds on their breath. They exist only to be witness to this moment.

He peels the t-shirt off and throws it into the backyard brambles. He spreads his legs. She sits between them, her black hair sticking between her back and his chest, dripping into his belly button and crotch. She stretches her legs out. Thunder implodes blackly. They wait for the next flash.

A dreadlocked head comes flinging out the bathroom window to their left. Her room-mate, Axe, says, "Ahhh, don't you guys look sweet, two little nature bunnies."

She flinches arms across her breasts and tenses. She becomes only tentatively present again. The head disappears and they slink in.

The next day sifts by grey, the sky a fine layer of dust. Outside in the West Annex, car stereos expand their volume in the heat and backyard voices try to rise above the noise in Greek, Italian, Spanish, Portuguese, Cantonese. Neither the heat nor the noise can animate the black room. An aura of decay hovers over the limp pillows. The gritty sheets reek of stale smoke, thick mucous, sticky sweat. Kisa wakes crumpled and stiff like an old dish rag.

She looks at Matt's slug-curled slumber, a chant whispering itself between her lips:

THERE'S NO WAY YOU CAN FEEL ME. THERE'S NO-
ONE WHO CAN HEAL ME. THERE'S NO PLACE TO
REACH YOU. THERE'S NOTHING TO TEACH YOU.
THERE'S NO WAY OUT.

She looks down at the list taped to the foot of the bed:

> 1. put in contact lenses
> 2. wash face
> 3. brush teeth
> 4. brush hair
> 5. make coffee
> 6. do tarot reading
> 7. plan what to do next

Without this list she used to spend at least an hour, if not
two, on waking just deciding in what order to accomplish
these daily duties.

She half-slides off the bed on to her hands. The safety pin
on her garter belt springs open and jabs into her thigh. She
slides all the way onto the floor before relieving this pain. She
tussles with the pile of black clothes around the bed like she
used to play with autumn leaves. Eventually, she finds a pair
of his grey underwear — his only non-black article — a
t-shirt that says "Eat the Rich", a long-line 'Fifties bra, and a
skirt cut short and trailing loose threads. She dresses, then
wanders into the hall. The bathroom door is locked and she
can hear the shower running. She closes the door to her
bedroom and sits with a sigh on the seat of an old formica
telephone table. She starts to count its gold stars.

One of the rubber bats hanging from the ceiling falls and flaps on Matt's forehead. It seems he is always awakened by something falling here. He is amazed at how much junk she has in this black hole. A stack of milk crates are crammed with tapes, books, clothes, jewelry, wigs, hats, make-up, antique cookie tins. These tins contain all kinds of treasures: freaks and serial killer trading cards, X-ray vision glasses, glow-in-the-dark Fimo clay for making skull and bone beads for necklaces, Jim Jones trading cards, lickum stickum tattoos, belly dancer finger cymbals, a broken Elvis watch, a toy TTC streetcar, a Three Wishes Voodoo Doll with a magic wand, horseback-riding camp ribbons, swimming and sailing badges, old love letters and school notes, and her dental x-rays. There is also a hatbox filled with the intricately engineered toys from inside chocolate Kinder eggs. The first thing she did after bringing him here was to show him all of her treasures. But when he'd ask how she acquired something, she'd only answer vaguely, "Oh, somebody gave it to me," or "I found it in a garbage."

An enormous trunk beside the bed is topped by a lamp, a red-eyed clock radio and a shrine to all the antique dolls of Kisa's childhood. Hanging above this is a bulletin board full of photographs.

These photographs don't seem to all belong to the same person. They are mostly of groups of people like families. Sometimes the same people are mixed up into different groupings. One group is sailing in crisp, white clothes. Another is horseback-riding in black jodhpurs and red suit-jackets. Then there is a group on a snowy slope wearing bright, tight ski suits. Although each of these pictures features mostly new characters, it always seems to be the same family. Interspersed among these images are photographs of denim-and-suede people around a fire in front of a teepee as the sun sets, naked people jumping off rocks and canoes into a mossy lake, and soggy people huddling on wet grass with guitars and African drums. At the centre of this collage is a blurry black-and-white picture of a man and a woman with a small child between them. The child is swinging between them, one hand in each of the adults' and her bare legs swinging in the air under a short skirt. This child he knows to be Kisa.

A long clothes rack stretches from the trunk all the way to the door. Here hangs a cornucopia of costumes: starchy prom dresses, lacy wedding gowns, medical uniforms, sequined evening dresses, velvet Edwardian capes, embroidered Tibetan mountain dresses, lederhosen, mirrored saris, and short black 'Fifties cocktail dresses. Kisa will come back soon to change her clothes and bring him coffee. He doesn't have much time.

Matt reaches under the mattress on her side, near the trunk. He pulls out a hard-covered black sketchbook. He discovered it when changing the sheets yesterday, the first time they'd been changed since he met her three months ago and moved in. It was a book of lists, in her cat-tail-swish handwriting. The lists were never completed with the same colour ink. He'd read the first two lists yesterday. He didn't understand why anyone would bother to record such trivialities. It intrigues him. She is still half a shadow to him. He wants to know what moves her grace. He suspects something lunar. Now here he's found something that could illuminate her, and it is absurdly banal. He reads the lists again.

#1 THINGS OTHER PEOPLE KNOW THAT I DON'T

    — how to keep fruits and vegetables fresh
    — how to polish shoes and boots
    — how to remove lint

— what Q-tips are for
— what baste means
— how to put on pantyhose without tearing it
— how to iron
— filling out forms
— driving
— how to shave your legs without cutting them

#2 THINGS I HAVE NEVER HAD

— pumice stone
— nail file
— dental floss
— blowdryer
— mop
— cookbook
— sweater shaver
— microwave
— a home

This last entry in the inane inventory of inadequacy seems to lift off the page as if surrounded by doodled stars and arrows. A clue. A word that also would be on his list, had he kept one. He'd been homeless when she'd found him at the film opening, homeless really for the last ten years. Since sixteen, he'd just been moving back and forth across the country with his stolen video camera. He'd wanted to shoot her when he first saw her but she refused. She still refuses. He doesn't know how to know her. And he has little more than these vain scribblings to decipher. He turns the page.

#3 BOOKS

- Dharma Bums by Jack Kerouac
- Beyond Good and Evil by Nietzche
- Blood and Guts in High School by Kathy Acker
- Tropic of Cancer by Henry Miller
- Pranks issue of RE/Search
- Exterminator by William S. Burroughs
- Selected Writings of Emma Goldman
- The Stranger by Camus
- Nausea by Sartre
- Concrete Island by J.G. Ballard
- The Ethics of Ambiguity by Simone de Beauvoir

#4 MOVIES

- The Great Rock'n'Roll Swindle
- Faster Pussycat Kill! Kill!
- Suburbia
- Basketcase
- Pink Flamingos
- Freaks
- Blue Velvet
- Smithereens
- Andy Warhol's Bad
- Eraserhead
- Subway
- Straight to Hell
- Betty Blue
- Diva

He is deflated. He puts the book back under the mattress, then wraps himself up in the covers again. He falls back asleep.

Kisa says good morning to the small woman with a double mohican sitting on the counter in a pink slip, Petra, who is trying to tear open the clear plastic safely sealing her Twinkies, but her hands are shaking. Kisa puts on the rubber boots in the doorway and wades through the huge grey puddle in the middle of the kitchen. The landlord has not come to fix the sink in five months, but the rent is too cheap to risk reporting her. Kisa takes the coffee out of the cupboard and dumps some into the cone. She puts the cone and some water into the coffee machine. It is so greasy that the brand name is completely obscured. She turns the machine on but the switch doesn't light up. It won't go. She hears Petra drop the plastic on the floor and asks her to help figure this out. With a twirl, Petra dangles the cord. "It's not plugged in."

Kisa plugs in the machine, then takes the boots off at the door to the livingroom. She puts her boots back on. Even though Matt cleaned it the other day, the livingroom is now ankle-deep in old newspapers, phone messages, beer bottles, pizza cartons. The wood floor had been used as an ashtray as the real ashtrays were spilling over everywhere. It was hopeless. They always talked about painting, but no-one even got to the point of taking the posters down from the yellowed walls. The posters reflected the destruction of the room — Sid Vicious shooting up, Edie Sedgewick after the Chelsea Hotel Fire, Iggy Pop exposing himself, Malcolm X, and the famous photograph of Jayne Mansfield's fatal car accident. Kisa lights a cigarette and sits down on a dining room chair found on the curb. The dining room had been given to Frank and Poppy's two pet ferrets after they had torn up the couch. Their smell still takes over the living room.

Kisa starts counting the little scars on her legs. Maybe if Matt got a job, they could afford a place of their own. She is used to living with boyfriends. Since she was fifteen she's lived with maybe eight of them. She is used to living with anybody. Sudden pop-n-fresh half-baked intimacies. Taking women she didn't really know to the hospital in the middle of the night as they bled profusely from their groins. Foiling suicide attempts by coming home early.

The coffee is ready. She puts in some whitener. They can't have milk because Mondo, who has the attic, pierced the freon when defrosting the freezer with a breadknife. She takes the two mugs upstairs and toes open her bedroom door. She sets them down on the floor, closes the door, then crawls onto the bed. Matt's hair prickles against the pillow. It is coming in a pine blonde. It had been purple but he shaved it for summer. She starts licking his broken nose to wake him up. He mumbles, "Hey, Pussycat."

She meows all silly and he opens his copper eyes. He runs his hand down her fishnets to where they are torn at the knee. The curl of his lips suggests a smile at all times, as they reach towards the wink lines of his eyes. He strokes her hair as she continues licking him down his skinny chest. She nips the slight beer belly that is not big enough to rise above his hipbones. He begins to tickle her, "Stop! The cof-fe-fe-fee is going to get cold." He brings their mugs over, resting them on the trunk as he lights cigarettes for himself and Kisa.

"What are we going to do about food?" he asks.

"I don't know, I don't get paid until the closing party tonight. Then we can go out. Somebody finished off our bread."

"I don't mind just eating the peanut butter with a spoon."

"Sure, go nuts. I don't want to eat until after the show."

She drains the last drop, puts out her cigarette and gets up.

She changes into a black cocktail dress and puts on battered black oxfords. "I'm going to do my tarot reading."

"Hope it bodes well."

"No. All I ever get is swords. Trouble and more trouble. Don't do anything, just wait it out."

"Well that storm last night must be a good sign."

"Maybe just a good moment," she smiles and turns to the door. He notices a split up the seam of her skirt, you can see she is wearing a garter belt.

As she goes downstairs, he puts on his black jeans and t-shirt. He has decided that her domestic incompetence is not mere laziness or inability. He deduces that it is her refusal to be in any way complicit with a target market group. She will not use detergents, accumulate unnecessary new objects, or waste time on things. It is enough for her to have the idea of all she has found or been given. The actual artifacts themselves just sit and collect dust. Even the things people have bought new for her so quickly become stained, grimy or torn that they never seem new. And he has never yet seen her in a store other than an all-night groceteria. He can't even imagine it. With these musings, he is drawn back to the scrapbook.

#5 THINGS TO FIX

> — sink
> — fridge
> — hematite necklace
> — zipper of purple feather dress
> — shoe-glue white go-go boots
> — paint bed gold
> — dye sheets black
> — clean EVERYTHING, you fucking slothgirl!
> — find dad's new address

#6 THINGS TO BUY IF I EVER GET MONEY

> — a stereo
> — gold stretch pants
> — some decent underwear
> — a red wagon
> — a Chinese tea basket
> — a home-brewing kit
> — 14-hole oxblood D.M.s
> —Szechuan peanut sauce
> — a small island in the South Pacific

#7 NOT-BAD JOBS

> — writing descriptions of flowers for a seed catalogue
> — phone-in psychic
> — making furniture out of scrap metal
> — ripping holes in old jeans for expensive store
> — Lost & Found Attendant
> — painting kinky cartoon people on nightclubs
> — contortionist
> — hermit

After the drain backed up with the contents of the entire street's sewage, including a rubber ball, a can of Coke and a diaphragm in the soup of excrement, nobody wanted the basement. So after the city drained it Kisa took it over. She burned a lot of incense and built a platform out of old wooden crates she'd scrounged. She walled the platform in with windows discarded at renovation sites. Heavy red drapery screens off her tarot table and the two cushions on either side. The table is very low and covered with black silk. There are two white candles at either end. Kisa lays the cards out. Her prediction of swords is correct, except there is an Ace of Wands in the position denoting Feelings of Others. The message is the beginning of fire, enterprise and distinction, in someone close to her. She doesn't have time to tell Matt. She runs upstairs, yells good-bye, grabs her bag, and tears out the door.

Matt is always disappointed that she never leaves time to kiss him. Kisa who does not kiss. He starts to fold and hang up the clothes crumpled on the floor. Then he collects the mugs and goes downstairs. He rinses the mugs in cold water and vinegar. The sink has given up on offering hot water to the puddle on the linoleum. He dries the mugs with a wine-stained tea towel and puts them in the cupboard. He has rolled up his jeans to step barefoot through the water. He takes some j-cloths and Nature Clean out of the broken fridge where he's hidden them. One by one, he takes Kisa's appliances out into the backyard and piles them carefully in a rusty shopping cart. Then he sits on a milkcrate and begins to clean the toaster oven. The sun hazes down and he hopes it will wash the pallor of his skin. He likes making things clean. Not like they are new but like they are appreciated. He would like to be someplace long enough to keep things clean. To feel he had a right to insist upon their cleanliness. He takes the toaster back in and begins on the popcorn maker, taking off his shirt as he starts to trickle from his armpits. He once asked her where all these machines had come from. She'd said, "Oh, one day a man came and put them on the porch. Then he drove away."

At first, he thought she was mysteriously alluding to some kind of sugar daddy. Which irritated him. Then he realized that she was talking about her real father, but in a mythic manner, The Appliance Man. At this point she elaborated, "I tried to call and thank him but the stepmother at that time said he'd moved out. And then I moved here so he probably can't find me. Maybe I have another stepmother. I don't know where he is."

At the theatre, Kisa lolls on a white-sheeted mattress in front
of the black curtain at the rear of the space. It has taken two
hours to have her body paint done. She is covered in flames.
Because she is behind the seats, the audience has to twist
around to see her. There are such tableaux throughout the
high-ceilinged narrow theater. She doesn't feel naked with the
body paint on. Nudity in front of the other cast members is
normal, because the troupe has worked together, clothed and
unclothed, for three years. Nudity in front of the audience is
a different matter. She always feels their eyes stripping something more from her in lieu of clothes. She feels the same way
when she has to pose for nude pictures to make rent in
between runs. Dutifully she drones her chant:

THERE'S NO WAY YOU CAN FEEL ME. THERE'S NO-
ONE WHO CAN HEAL ME. THERE'S NO PLACE TO
REACH YOU. THERE'S NOTHING TO TEACH YOU.
THERE IS NO WAY OUT.

She does this for two hours, until the crescendo of all the
chants rises and she begins shrieking it — an alley opera. The
silent man in black at front stage centre begins climbing the
stairs in that go straight up in front of him, into and past the
audience. He is carrying a torch. When her vocalization tran-
scends linguistics, he sets fire to the side of the bed facing the
audience. Behind the bonfire, she does a quick roll off the other
side of the bed and slips under the curtain. There she straightens and begins wiping off the smeared greasepaint, gritty with
dust. The theatre is too low-budget for showers, so she makes
do with a basin of water and a few washcloths. She puts on a
robe and sneaks out the back door. She prowls around the side

of the theatre, avoiding shards of glass, goes through the deserted lobby and down the stairs to the dressing room.

She knows that if she thinks about her work she might have to shrug or perform some similar ritual of derision, might have to figure out what, if anything, it does or means. So she doesn't think about it. Sometimes she reads her name following the term actress in a small review in NOW Magazine and it gives her a vague sense of purpose. It is a comfort of some kind, as is being able to leave the rest of it — how to move, what to say, what it means, what it is worth — up to others.

Matt is finally finished with his chore when the sun begins to set. The horizon glows with an acidic urban green in between buildings. The same green as Kisa's eyes after she has camouflaged her pond irises with coloured contacts. He fetches both last night's and today's t-shirts from the stiff weeds and washes them in the kitchen sink. He wrings them and hangs them on the kitchen clothesline so that they drip into the puddle. It is almost time for the closing party. He puts on overalls, takes a token from her jar, and goes to the theater to meet her.

Matt sees her in the lobby talking to a shorter man in a white swashbuckler's shirt and tight black pants. He has dark hair in a little ponytail at the nape. It's Dag. Matt has been looking for him for weeks. Matt kisses Kisa and slips his arm around her. "You found Dag!"

Dag thinks they are a strange couple. Both tall, they look like stretched-out versions of Howdy Doody and Betty Boop. Dag kisses Matt on the cheek, then turns back to Kisa. "Yeah, so it was FUBAR. I just stared at the director like DILLIGAF and fired him. I mean, BFD, right? It's my fucking grant."

"What?" says Kisa, not having spent time on the West coast.

"He said that it was Fucked Up Beyond All Repair, so he

gave the Do I Look Like I Give A Fuck death-stare, Big Fucking Deal," Matt translates easily and turns to Dag. "What are
you talking about?"

"Oh, I got a big grant to do that film we workshopped
together because I raised some corporate funds. Since you were
Not To Be Found, I got this guy Justin to go in and he just
fucked everything up. But now that I've found you, we'll take a
Fucking Big Hammer to it and fix it up. There's even a salary
for you, Matt, but it's a tight schedule, which is why I needed
someone right away. Here, I'll give you my new address."

Kisa slips away to get more cheap champagne. She wants a
shower badly. Her hair reeks of smoke. She sways back to Matt
and Dag. They are ranting rapid-fire. She rubs her nose against
Matt's shoulder. He turns to her in mid-sentence and she
whispers, "I'm going, stay if you want."

"You haven't made me a key, yet. I'll go with you."

"No, you can climb up the back into the window. I'll leave
it open."

"No, really, I'd rather go now. Last time I broke the trellis
on the shed, fell on my ass and slept in the shopping cart,"
Matt is laughing, "I'll see you tomorrow, Dag."

Kisa is already walking out the door. He catches up to her.
They decide to walk home. She hasn't eaten but isn't hungry.

"Tomorrow I'll take you out for breakfast. Was Dag seri-
ous? You really have a job? Or is he as full of shit as he seems?"

"Oh, come on, you don't even know the guy. He's alright.
I think it's funny the way he plays that shit up."

"You like everybody."

"So what? I like you best. And now I can pay my fair share
and get out of your hair."

"If it works out."

As they curl together, both wishing for another storm, some moment that can make them meet, she is restless and kicking off the sheets. "It was so nice today after the rain last night cooled everything down. I'm so hot I could scream."

"Kind of a repeat performance, Pussycat. Aren't you tired?"

"Yeah, but I wish I had a fan," she pauses, "Maybe you could tell me a story, something funny."

"Okay, let me think a minute," he lights a cigarette, "did you used to do pills when you were younger?"

"Sure. I carried all different kinds in this bubble from a supermarket toy machine. Me and my best friend would just plop five or so down without even looking. Sometimes I would get really hyper and she would get really zonked. Sometimes the opposite."

"Well, I was hanging out with my best friend, who later killed himself. We were living together in this industrial dive. We'd dropped out of grade nine and all we did was work the late shift at 7-11 and then drink all day. This one day we drank way way way too much. We went over to this girl's place instead of showing up for work. She was having a party. We just took everything handed to us. Then I went into the bathroom and took everything in the medicine chest. The next thing I knew I was in the hospital. My friend, Mike, had brought the empty vials down. I saw them on the night-table," Matt starts laughing and slaps his forehead, "They were mostly acne pills! And here was this doctor trying to talk to me about suicide! It was hilarious, yeah, I'm such a pathetic mess I tried to off myself with acne pills!"

He is still laughing, but she isn't. "Is that true?"

"Well, it really happened. But I wasn't trying to die. I was just too drunk. Don't take this too seriously. It's a joke."

"I'm just surprised. You seem so happy all the time. Even if you weren't trying to die, it was pretty self-destructive. When I'm like that it's because I feel miserable, like I can't find myself anyway, so why not lose myself as much as I can."

"No, it wasn't like that. I was just going whole hog. Shhh. Go to sleep. I'm sorry my story wasn't funny to you." He kisses her forehead.

As soon as she begins snoring, he fetches the scrapbook from its hiding place and reads it, holding up his lighter. There are pages of tickets for gigs under the heading #8 BANDS I'VE SEEN. He lists them to himself: Agnostic Front, Youth Youth Youth, Young Lions, The Ugly, Hype, Fifth Column, Direct Action, Mike Marley and the Sailors, VBF, Body Bag, Norda, Bratty and the Babysitters, Jolly Tambourine Man, Prisoners of Conscience, Rentboys Inc, the Viletones, Blibber and the Rat Crushers, Madhouse, Meatwagon, Vos Ist Los, Suckerpunch, BFG, Vital Sines, Living Proof, UIC, DRI, No Mind, Chronic Submission, Handsome Ned, Poison Girls, Chicken Milk, Suicidal Tendencies. Then there is an addendum: "Actually, these are only the tickets I found in my old jacket."

#9 PLACES I LIKED TO GO TO

> — The Edge
> — The Turning Point
> — Larry's Hideaway
> — the DMZ
> — the Batcave
> —Voodoo
> — Frankenstein's
> — Pariah
> — Ildiko's
> — Quoc Té

Then there is a list so extensive that she hadn't bothered to organize the names in neat columns. His lighter is burning his fingers. He takes the book into the bathroom and sits on the toilet. After a few seconds of squinting, his eyes adjust to the light, although sore from the effort.

#10 TAPES

Generation X, X, X-ray Specs, Trotsky Icepick, Social Distortion, the Del Fuegos, the Misfits, Bad Brains, the Germs, Crucifux, Crucifix, the Descendants, TSOL, firehose, the Fleshtones, the Undertones, the Minutemen, Subhumans, Clitboys, Crass, Effigies, Flux of Pink Indians, the Demics, Redd Kross, Pavement, Minor Threat, Siouxie and the Banshees, Bauhaus, The Cramps, the Violent Femmes, The Damned, Stiff Little Fingers, Killing Joke, Gun Club, the Stranglers, the Dead Kennedys, the Fall, Alien Sex Fiends, Dayglo Abortions, GBH, the Dickies, Articles of Faith, Sisters of Mercy, the Slits, Fear, the Pogues, Flipper, Buzzcocks, Psychic TV, the Swans, Mortal Coil, Big Black, Joy Division, Ministry, Dead Can Dance, UK Subs, the Revolting Cocks, Eisensturzen Neuboten, Cocteau Twins, Black Flag, the Butthole Surfers, Millions of Dead Cops, DOA, Jesus & Mary Chain, Corrosion of Conformity, Sonic Youth, Dag Nasty, Crass, SexGangChildren, Tav Falco & Panther Burns, Tones On Tail, PIL, Death Horror Inc.

Why would she bother writing all this down and hiding it? What does she need such an archive for? Maybe it is simply an inventory in case one of the roommates steals some of her tapes. His eyes are burning. He is very careful stealing into the bedroom and replacing the book. She is no longer snoring. He touches her eyelids gently, the whisk of a wing. All is still.

He is never there any more. He leaves before she wakes, except the couple of days she works as a movie extra. She is grabbing odd jobs. Posing for life drawing classes, replacing absent beer servers, he doesn't know what all. Late at night he steals the book to alleviate his caffeine quaking in the bathroom. The writing is increasingly chaotic.

#11 HIP THANGS (ugh)

wearing slips as dresses, chains and safety pins, motorcycle boots, Thrift Villa, Crazy Color and Manic Panic hairdye, dog collars and bondage gear, tattoos and piercings, bisexuality and asexuality, crabs and chlamydia, acid and heroin, pet snakes and rats, IPA beer and Drum tobacco, skulls & anarchy symbols, Maximum Rock'n'Roll fanzine, Kick It Over anarchist paper, the Animal Liberation Front, veganism, garbage-picking and graffiti, BFI (biffy) bins, all night donut shops, "Iggy Pop is God", "Evol, Evol, Evol", conspiracy theories, Andy Boy box labels, religious paraphernalia, roadkills in jars, suicide...

After that the book seems to end. He keeps checking it. After about a month of stepped-up production on the film, he discovers a new list.

#12 DISAPPEARED PEOPLE

> — Camellia went to art school in Montreal
> — Scuzz got arrested for drugs and went to jail
> — Rudy hung himself or jumped in front of a subway car (rumour)
> — Cindy was hospitalized for anorexia

— Carlos went to fight for the revolution in
  Guatemala, ha, ha
— Rene died of a heroin overdose
— Jules and Layla went treeplanting in B.C.
— Patty went to Sudbury and had a baby
— Zoe moved to a squat in Seattle
— Suzy became a survivalist and built a treehouse in
  the Rockies
— Mom went to the ashram in Washington State
— who knows where Dad is
—

This last unfinished dash unnerves him. Is she waiting for
him to disappear, or is she getting rid of him? Lately, like
tonight, he gets to her bed over the arch of midnight and it is
empty. By morning, she is always curled in a ball at his feet,
but he has to leave before she stretches out and opens her eyes.
His only knowledge of her comes from the book now. Does
she suspect? At any rate, the time has come to tell her that he
has broken into her lists, even if he has not yet broken their
code. He takes a pen and writes:

Kisa, my pussycat,

I have been reading this book of yours. Please don't get
mad. We never see each other. I want to know you.
Soon we can talk.

Suddenly, he wants to scratch it out. It sounds too simple.
He can't code the feeling in words. If he could film it, he
would shoot a white swan rising out of a black sea. As the
swan spread its wings in the night sky, it would shed its white
feathers one by one until the swan was as black as the sea and

the sky. The swan would be identical to where it was and where it had come from. Then it would grow new feathers — red ones, like petals, like flames. That is how he sees it. But the image explains nothing. He is dreaming of swans when she comes in to curl at his feet.

When she wakes alone, she stretches across the bed, then slides on to the floor in her usual fashion. Kisa is beginning to enjoy mornings alone. She doesn't have to talk. What she does now is go through her treasures or her trunk. The trunk is home to her childhood. There rests her Pippi Longstocking and Harriet the Spy, her Oz and Narnia. Some of her old clothes are there too. Her baby dresses, smocked by her great-grandmother, her tiny tie-dyed t-shirts and patched jeans, her embroidered sack dresses, and her denim replica of a motorcycle jacket. She is saving these for her future children. There are also toys: Tonka trucks, a Fisher Price camper, Lego, the Sunshine family, and an anatomically correct African-American male doll. Then there are the educational toys from her father: a model of the human brain, a microscope, Edward De Bono's Five-Day Course in Thinking, brain teaser cards, a globe, and her prize possession — his old copy of ee cummings' 100 Selected Poems.

Kisa takes out the globe, puts everything else back carefully, closes the trunk and replaces the lamp, clock, and antique dolls. She sips her lukewarm coffee and idly spins the globe. Then she takes out her scrapbook. She is not surprised to see his message. She didn't care if he was reading her book. She wouldn't write anything too revealing because she knows eventually it would come into prying hands. The "I want to know you. Soon we'll talk" phrases simply confirm what she is already suspecting. They will talk and he will say, "I want us to be friends." They just managed to skip the "I need space" part because he got a job. Once again the Coming Together will flip to the Falling Apart. And then one of them will move.

She writes:

#13   PLACES I WANT TO GO TO

— Tallahassee
— Phoenix
— Amsterdam
— Venice
— Kampala
— Mozambique
— Sri Lanka
— Caracas
— Head Smashed In Buffalo Jump

Basically she wants to be someone else being someplace else. Here she feels to be anywhere. Herself she feels to be anybody. Once she had a place and it was someplace, she had a body and it was somebody. Now she has been anybody anywhere for so long that she can't remember any more what it was like. To belong to a place, to belong to people. From there to here was a dervish dance. If she was to trace her staying places across Toronto chronologically, the pattern would form a crazy web, something to get confused in, stuck in. She writes a bit more and then she goes out.

All day she rides the TTC and walks until her sandals have branded her feet with criss-crossing welts. She goes first to Yorkville and sees the hairdressing salon. Then she goes to Cabbagetown and sees the lawn cobblestoned over. Next, she goes to Forest Hill and sees the tree grown. In the Beaches, the peace sign has been painted over. She hasn't the security clearance to get into the waterfront condo. She retraces the separate paths of her parents and then she begins on her own. She visits Regent Park, Kensington Market, Queen St. West, Little Portugal. She sees warehouses and parking lots where they'd had a van and old yellow brick apartment buildings with thin windows and patterns painted on the walls that make you walk tipsy. It is almost the next morning before she finishes the entire route and stumbles up the broken wooden steps of her house in the West Annex.

It is as if she has etched a connect-the-dots picture deeper into her, like prehistoric rock carvings in the depths of mazing caves, the effort of the transcription alone granting significance to her etchings and, by extension, to her, the possessor, the creator. She falls asleep dreaming of dancing ochre bison and bull jumpers lining her uterine walls.

Matt has a horrible thought, maybe it is she who will disappear. Maybe he will go back to the house and not only will she not be there but all her stuff will be gone. He can see himself entering the dark room to flop on the bed and landing instead on the dusty, black floor. It would be like sinking into a grave. No, she has too much junk to move suddenly. Unless. Unless, she was seeing someone else and surreptitiously moving piece by piece into the new lover's place. Newton's First Law of Motion: the momentum of a body is unchanged unless it is acted upon by some external force. He can't repress his urge to go straight home after the dailies instead of hashing out the details in his meticulous fashion. When he gets home, she is not there.

Everything seems in its place, but there are so many things, maybe he just can't tell. He sits on the edge of the bed and lights a cigarette. Then he reaches under the mattress and frees the book. He reads the first new entry and begins to panic, she is leaving him. Then he reads the last list. #14 WHERE I HAVE BEEN AND WITH WHO. This house is not on the list. It, and by extension, him, are not yet in the past tense. He doesn't know what she is trying to do, what she is telling him. The list is confusing, too many names he doesn't recognize. She is in one house until she is ten then she is everywhere at once.

He wants to find her right away. He sets out to search every nightclub and boozecan on both Bloor and Queen. Laplace: if we know a single point in phase space then we can determine the future motion of a body and also calculate how that body will collide and interact with other bodies. Suddenly, he knows what the scrapbook of lists is. It is a map. She is trying to situate herself. Maybe he can trace the path she makes to find her, maybe even to know her some.

She wakes up because he lands on her feet and it hurts. He is mumbling, "You call this piece of shit coffee? I'd rather drink from the dick of a goat!" and laughing. She is trying to wriggle her feet out from under his back, but right when she gets one free he grabs one of her ankles. She pries his fingers off and slides to the floor. One by one she undoes the nine buckles on his motorcycle boot. It takes a standing-up pull to yank it off. She unbuckles the next one but falls on her ass, tugging it off because he starts kicking. He is still singing that Killdozer lyric over and over and laughing. She unbuttons his black jeans and tries to pull them off but they get bunched up above his bent knee, so she gives up. He looks pretty foolish like that, so she decides to do the same to his t-shirt, leaving it twisted around his neck and shoulders. That will get him. He will feel like a complete jackass when he wakes up. She starts to slide the shirt up. As soon as it gets under his armpits, she notices a white bandage on the left side of his chest.

Her first thought is that he has gotten himself stabbed. Slowly, she peels back the white tape holding the gauze down. There is dried blood in crusty crests. She dips the bottom of her black slip in the glass of water on the floor. He is snoring loudly now. She dabs at the dried blood. Underneath is a brighter red. She keeps dabbing. At the center of a rose's mouth is the initial K. The K is sculpturally baroque in purple and gold. A gold fork of lightning is striking it, outlining its arrow-head angles in splitting hairs, loose threads of lightning that kindle the flaming petals. The tattoo is beginning to scab over. The edges of the floral maze are browning.

She smoothes the bandage back in place. Then she pulls the t-shirt down over it, patting it gently over the soft cloth. At least he made it home. She goes back to work pulling off his jeans.

Jennifer Duncan is a fifth generation Torontonian so she walks too fast, talks too much and won't hug people she doesn't know. She earned her BA in English and Creative Writing at York University and won the President's Prize for Prose. She earned her MA in English and Creative Writing at Concordia University in Montreal where *Sanctuary & Other Stories* won the David McKeen Award for best creative writing thesis. Her poetry and prose have been published in *Matrix, Prairie Fire, Contemporary Verse 2,* and *Blood & Aphorisms,* who included her in their first anthology. She contributes book reviews to *NOW Magazine, Quill & Quire, Books In Canada* and *The National Post.* She has taught writing at The City School, The Avenue Road School of the Arts, George Brown College and Concordia University. She possesses an inordinate number of toys and has a small play therapy practice. She no longer has spraypainted walls or milkcrate furniture but she still scavenges biffy bins and catches the odd gig.

JENNIFER DUNCAN
Photograph by Elizabeth Gold